THE SINGING TREE

THE SINGING TREE

Caryl Porter

CROSSWAY BOOKS • WESTCHESTER, ILLINOIS
A DIVISION OF GOOD NEWS PUBLISHERS

This book is for Valerie Lisa Robbins

With special thanks to
The Rt. Rev'd Michael Ball, C.G.A., Bishop of Jarrow,
who graciously consented to step into the story.

The Singing Tree. Copyright © 1989 by Caryl
Porter. Published by Crossway Books, a division of
Good News Publishers, Westchester, Illinois 60154.

Cover illustration: Wm Neal McPheeters

Cover design: Jack Jewell

First printing, 1989

Printed in the United States of America

Library of Congress Catalog Card Number 88-63693

ISBN 0-89107-520-8

Ariel Marsden did not know that she was dreaming. The things she saw were so terrible that she tried to close her eyes, but she could not. In her dream she was forced to look.

Her home was destroyed, her huge oak tree blackened and dead. Silence hung over a desolate landscape. She was stunned, unable to move.

Then, in her dream, she saw someone moving toward her. It was a young man. Ariel had never seen a man so handsome. No, she thought, not handsome. Beautiful. He radiated light.

She knew he was not an ordinary man. In one way she wanted to run to him; in another she was afraid. But in her dream she was unable to move. She was caught in a terrible dark silence beside the dead oak tree.

Then the shining man spoke to her. "Do not be afraid, Ariel. I have come to help you."

The dream faded. Ariel turned over, reached for her bear, Gladly, sighed, and snuggled down into her covers. Once again she slept deeply.

1

"Won't it be wonderful?" Ariel Marsden looked at her best friend, Robin. They sat together on the deck of the swimming pool at Robin's house. The California sun warmed them, the pool water was clear and blue, and the end of school was only two weeks away.

"It's going to be fantastic," Robin said. "How are we going to wait nearly five weeks?"

"I know. But that isn't so terribly long and we still have a lot to do. I'm so glad your mom is going to let us swim here."

"Me too." Robin grinned at her friend. "Have you asked him yet?"

"No. Not yet. But I'm going to. Maybe on Monday. I've asked Matt and Janice and Kim. But not Kevin. Do you really think he'll come?"

"Sure. Why not?"

"Do you think six people is a good number for a party? Our patio isn't big enough for more than six people."

"It's a perfect number," Robin assured her. Then she asked, "Want some lemonade?"

"OK."

"I'll be right back." Robin went into the house.

Ariel thought about the plans she had made for her thirteenth birthday party on the seventh of July. She was sure Kevin would come if she invited him. He liked her. She could tell. She loved to think about the way it had begun.

She had felt her ankle fold under her in the hall one morning on the way to class. She had fallen and it hurt so much that she couldn't stand up. Almost before she knew what was happening, Kevin had knelt beside her.

"What happened?" he asked.

"It's my ankle. I guess I can't walk."

He had picked her up as if she were a feather and carried her to the nurse's office. She had put her arms around his neck and laid her face against his chest. She had almost forgotten how much her ankle hurt.

After that day she was sure he looked at her in a different way than he had before. After all, she was only a seventh grader, and seventh-grade girls usually didn't even exist for eighth-grade boys.

"Here." Robin handed her a glass of lemonade and put a basket of corn chips on the table.

"Thanks." Ariel reached for some chips. "Wait till I tell you what he said today," she said dreamily.

"Who?"

"Kevin, of course. I can't believe what he said."

"Well, tell me." Robin sounded impatient.

"He said, 'I'll bet you look gorgeous in a swimsuit.'"

Robin let out her breath in a slow whistle. "He said that?"

"He really did." Ariel knew she wasn't exactly gorgeous, but interesting things were happening to her body and she had hope.

"What suit will you wear?" Robin asked. "To the party, I mean."

"A new one. I've already got it. It's a sort of silver-blue. I love it." She looked at Robin. "I wish I looked like you. You really do look gorgeous in a swimsuit. Do you suppose I will by my birthday?"

"Maybe. Probably." Robin was always encouraging.

She had a lovely figure and she never teased Ariel about the fact that she didn't yet.

Ariel thought Robin's blonde wavy hair and her dark brown eyes were beautiful. Again she said, "I wish I looked like you. I hate my hair. It's so straight. And I hate my freckles."

Robin studied her friend. "I've told you before. You're pretty. When you wear your hair like that, brushed straight back with a band and with the ends curled under, you look great. And your eyes are so different. They aren't just blue and they aren't brown and they aren't green. Sort of a little bit of everything."

"Speckled," Ariel said with disgust.

"No. What does your father call them? You told me once."

"Hazel."

"Yes. That's it. Well," Robin said, "anyway, I think you're pretty."

"Thanks," Ariel said. "But I'd still rather look like you."

Robin shrugged. "Let's talk about something else. This is embarrassing. Let's talk about your party. First we'll swim here. Then the girls can change in my room and the boys can use the cabaña. Right?"

"Right." Ariel was excited just at the prospect of her party. "Then we'll go to my house for supper. My cake is going to have white frosting with pink roses. Kind of like a wedding cake. And my father's going to make ice cream for us."

"Fantastic," Robin said. "He makes the world's best ice cream."

"Then we'll listen to music in the patio. You can bring some of your tapes so we'll be sure to have enough. Oh, Robin, it's going to be so special."

Robin said slowly, "What if Kevin says he can't come?"

Ariel stared at her. "What do you mean? Of course

he'll come." They were quiet for a long moment. Then Ariel asked plaintively, "Won't he?"

"Sure he will." Robin sighed. "Five whole weeks to wait."

Ariel asked suddenly, "What time is it?"

Robin looked at her watch. "Ten of four."

"I've got to go." Ariel swallowed the rest of her lemonade. "My father gets home early on Fridays. Maybe we're going out to dinner. I'll call you later."

"OK." Robin walked toward the gate with her. "Want me to go partway with you?"

"If you want to. You don't have to, though."

"OK. I'll talk to you later then. Have fun tonight."

"Thanks." Ariel rode her bike home thinking that she had never been quite so happy. As she rode into her driveway she looked up at the oak tree whose branches spread above the house, the garage, and even part of the street.

"I'm home," she told the tree. It had been Ariel's friend as long as she could remember. She climbed it often. When she sat in the fork of its boughs she felt that she was part of the tree itself.

She had a secret about the tree, one she had never told anyone.

Sometimes the tree sang.

Its voice was not at all like a human voice. It was more beautiful than any sound she had ever heard. She could not understand the words, but the melody it sang was real and Ariel could sing it, too. When they sang together Ariel felt, up in its high branches, that not only was she a part of the tree but part of the sky, too. A part of everything.

Now as she stood looking at the tree, a young man came out of Ariel's house and walked toward her. His hair was blond, even more blond than Robin's, and it was rather long. It framed his face and turned under at his collar.

In a moment they stood face to face and looked at each other. The young man's eyes were so dark that it seemed to Ariel she looked through them into a deep, mysterious space. She shivered.

"Don't be afraid," he said.

And all at once she wasn't.

He smiled at her and she felt warmed. "That's a remarkable tree," he said.

"Yes. My father says it's over a hundred years old."

"That's a relatively long time," the stranger said. Ariel thought she caught a glimmer of amusement in his eyes. She didn't know what he thought was funny. Then he said, "We both know that your tree is rare and wondrous. Good-bye, Ariel. We'll meet again."

How does he know all that? she wondered. *I've never told anybody about the tree. And how did he know my name?*

She watched him walk away. The sun shone on his hair, making a golden glow all around him. She watched until he was out of sight. Something about him was familiar. Then she remembered. She remembered her dream. She laid her hand against the rough bark of the oak tree, feeling its strength, looking up into the mesh of its leaves. The man who knew her name, who told her not to be afraid, was exactly like the man in her dream.

She found her parents sitting together in the patio. They weren't talking. They were just looking at each other. She thought they looked surprised. Or stunned, as if they had had bad news. A pang of fear shot through her.

"What's wrong?" she asked. "Who was that man?"

Her mother turned to look at her. "Hello, darling." The blue dress she wore made her eyes look even more blue than usual. A slight breeze lifted her dark hair.

"Who was that man?" Ariel asked again.

"His name is Mr. Herauld," her father told her.

"What did he want? He's different. He even knew my name. Did you tell him?" She didn't mention her dream.

Her parents looked at each other and again Ariel couldn't decide what they were thinking. "Please tell me," she begged. "What did he want?"

"He brought us some rather surprising news," her father told her. Then abruptly he asked, "Have you had a good day?"

Ariel knew he was changing the subject, but she said, "Yes. Robin and I have been talking about my party. It's going to be absolutely super."

Again that look passed between her parents. Then her mother said, "Tell her, Hugh."

Right away Ariel knew something awful was going to happen. "What is it? Is it something about my birthday?"

"In a way," her father said. "I'm afraid we won't be celebrating it here after all. We'll be in France. We're leaving for Europe right after school is out."

Ariel stared at her parents. For a moment she forgot about the stranger. She was too surprised, too shocked to speak. Then she said, "Well, I can't go. I have to be here. It's all planned."

Her mother's tone was sympathetic. "We know how you feel about your party and about this summer. We're really sorry to have to change your plans. It will still be a special summer, but in a different way."

Ariel clutched at possibilities. "Couldn't I stay with Robin while you two go? I know Robin's mom wouldn't mind. We're together all the time anyway."

"Ariel . . ." Her father sounded very serious. "It's nothing we can change. We all have to go." Then he smiled at her. "A trip to Europe can't be all that bad, can it?"

"I don't care about Europe." Ariel was growing more angry and upset by the minute. "I've got my birthday

party all planned. The thirteenth one is really important. And you both said I could plan the whole thing.
Besides, I have to be here for . . . well, for lots of things."
For Kevin, she thought, *now that he's begun to notice
me.*

Then something in the way her parents looked at her
made her afraid. "Daddy, please tell me. What's going
on?"

Her father said, "I can tell you this much. Mr. Herauld came especially to talk to us. He says we must go.
In a way, he gave us our orders."

"Well, who is he anyway?" Ariel remembered the
strength she had seen in the stranger's face. And she
thought of the way his eyes had looked—eyes with
dark, mysterious depths. As if a cloud had passed over
the sun, blotting it out, she was suddenly cold. She ran
to her father and he held her close. The man in her
dream and Mr. Herauld had both told her not to be
afraid. But she was. She couldn't help it. She was
afraid.

2

Waking the next morning, Ariel was vaguely aware
that something unpleasant had happened. Then she
remembered what it was. She held her bear, Gladly,
and lay in bed thinking of the party she was not going
to have.

As if she were watching a movie with herself as the
star, she followed the scenes. The six of them swimming in Robin's pool, she in her new suit. Coming back
to her house for supper. Her beautiful cake. Music in
the patio, Ariel wearing the long dress which was to be
her main gift. It was white with narrow straps and an
embroidered band at the hem. She sighed.

"Ariel?" Her mother called to her.

"I'm awake."

"Breakfast. Blueberry pancakes."

They were Ariel's absolute favorite. She went to the
kitchen where her mother sat sipping coffee while her
father made the pancakes.

"Hi," he greeted her. "How many?"

"Three, I guess. Did you get a chance to talk about
the trip?" she asked them. "Can you tell me about it
now?" She buttered her pancakes and poured syrup on
them. They smelled wonderful.

"Yes. We've made some plans. We'll leave here on
the evening of your last day of school," her father said.

Ariel felt her stomach lurch. She'd even miss the

school party. "I thought you had to have a passport to go to Europe," she said. "I don't have one."

"Mr. Herauld is making special arrangements," her father told her. "We gave him copies of your class picture."

"It's horrible."

"It's not that bad," her mother protested.

But Ariel scowled, resentment boiling inside her.

"At any rate," her father went on, "we'll fly directly to London and stay a few days there. I'm sure you'll like London."

Ariel asked, "Will we see Princess Di?"

"You never know." Her father smiled. "Then we're going to explore some of the great cathedrals in England." He glanced at Ariel's mother. Ariel couldn't quite translate the look which passed between them.

"Then where?" she asked.

"To Paris for a few days." He slid some pancakes onto his wife's plate. "And next we'll go to the small city of Chartres"—he pronounced it *Shart'ruh*—"southwest of Paris. One of the great buildings of the world is there. The cathedral. *Notre Dame de Chartres.*"

Again that look passed between her parents. She knew both of them so well that she could usually tell what they were thinking. But she could not interpret this particular look. Recognition was part of it, she thought, and agreement. And fear. What could her parents be afraid of? Although they were cheerful, talking about ordinary things, she was sure they didn't really feel cheerful.

"Something's wrong, isn't it?" she asked them. "And you aren't telling me. You're going to drag me away and you won't tell me why. It isn't fair."

"We'll tell you when we can," her father said. "We're not permitted to tell you yet. Meanwhile, there's nothing at all wrong with the trip itself. Especially if you can feel right about it."

Ariel said, "Well, I can't. Not if I can't be here on my birthday."

"We know how you feel," her mother said.

Ariel was stubborn. "I don't think you do." Then she asked, "May I go and tell Robin?"

"Of course."

She put Gladly in her bike basket and rode the three blocks to Robin's house. Leaning the bike against the wall near the back door she whistled their special signal, the first four notes of the Beethoven Fifth.

Robin looked out the kitchen window. "Hi."

"Come on out. I have something terrible to tell you."

Robin looked at Ariel in dismay. "Bad news? You aren't terminally sick with some ghastly disease, are you?"

"No. It isn't anything like that. Come on. Let's sit by the pool."

They walked out to the pool deck and sat together looking at the water. It was peaceful there. "It isn't your folks, is it?" Robin asked. "They aren't getting a divorce, are they?"

Almost all their classmates had been through at least one divorce. Robin's own parents had separated long ago. The closest thing Robin had to a father was her eighteen-year-old brother, Ned. He still lived at home. He was Robin's favorite person, after her mother.

"It isn't that," Ariel told Robin. "But it's awful, just the same. I won't be here for my birthday. We're going to Europe. I won't even be here for the class party. We're leaving that night."

Robin stared at her. "That's terrible. You have it all planned. Kevin and everything."

Robin always understood. "Yes," Ariel said. "Everything."

Robin asked impulsively, "Couldn't you stay here with me? My mom wouldn't care. You're here most of the time anyway, when I'm not at your house."

"I know." Ariel swallowed hard. "I already thought of that. But they say I have to go with them."

Robin sighed. "That marvelous party! Why do they have to go to Europe, anyway?"

"I'm not sure. It's something weird. This man came to see them. Mr. Herauld. I wish you could see him. He's . . . " But somehow she couldn't tell Robin about him. She wasn't sure what her friend would think about a man so unusual that it was impossible to describe him.

"Well, anyway, I think it's something about my father's work," Ariel said. "Something about cathedrals. Whatever it is, we have to go, and I won't be here."

"It's terrible," Robin said again.

"I know. I just can't believe it. And I'm sort of worried because they aren't telling me everything."

"Parents are strange," Robin said thoughtfully. "I remember the way mine acted when they were deciding to get the divorce. They didn't tell us what was going on. But we knew something was wrong. You can feel it."

"Yes." Ariel held Gladly against her face and felt his smooth fur. It comforted her just to hold him.

Robin watched her. Then she said, "I've always meant to ask you. Why did you name that bear of yours Gladly? That's a crazy name for a bear."

Ariel laughed in spite of herself. "Daddy named him. I've had him since I was about four, I guess. Look at him. He's sort of cross-eyed."

"He sure is." Robin crossed her own eyes and made a horrible face.

"Stop that. You'll ruin your eyes," Ariel scolded. "Anyway, Daddy named him Gladly, the cross-eyed bear. Get it?"

Robin looked blank. "No."

"Oh, you know. It's that hymn. 'Gladly the cross I'd bear.' "

Robin said with disgust, "That's sick." But she laughed. "Are you going to drag that poor bear all the way to Europe?"

"Of course I am. I never go anyplace without him. You know that. And now he has to go to Europe."

Robin reached to pat him. "Poor old bear."

"Oh, Robin, sometimes I think I just can't stand it. To go away, I mean. How can they make me do it when they know how much I want to be here?" Ariel looked at her friend as if Robin might have an answer for her.

But Robin only said, "I don't know. Parents can do anything they want to, I guess. Mine did when they split up. I couldn't stop that. I guess you can't stop this, either."

"I guess not." Ariel sighed. "But I feel terrible. Everything's gone wrong."

Robin looked at her and said, "Not everything. You've still got a mother *and* a father."

Ariel knew what her friend was thinking. "I just don't understand it," she said. "Sometimes everything's so sad."

3

The next Saturday morning Ariel put Gladly in her bike basket and rode over to Robin's house. She leaned her bike against the kitchen wall and whistled their special signal.

Robin came to the door at once. "Hi."

Ariel stared at her. "What have you been doing to yourself, for heaven's sake? You look exactly like Dorrie Mae, all but your hair."

Dorrie Mae was in their class. Her black hair was permed into long, tight curls. She wore close-fitting sweaters which made her look like a TV star and about twenty years old. One was electric blue with silver sequins at the neck. Another was white with a red heart appliqued over her own heart. She wore makeup to school. Lots of it. One day she had worn thick, curling false lashes. Mr. Long had talked to her at recess time and she took them off. But she still used mascara on her own lashes.

Now Robin batted her eyes at Ariel and said in a voice like Dorrie Mae's, low and sultry, "Do, do come in." They both grinned.

Ariel went with Robin to her bedroom and saw the makeup spread out on the dressing table. "What do you think?" Robin asked. "Really?"

"Are you serious?"

Robin sighed. "I was kind of experimenting. All the magazines say that a woman has an obligation to make the most of her assets and improve her weak points. I'm just trying."

"Are you planning to wear it to school?" Ariel asked.

Then Robin laughed, and suddenly she seemed to be herself again. "I wouldn't have the nerve. Besides, it's dumb. If you put it on, you have to take it all off again. Pam says you absolutely have to get it all off every night or your skin goes bad. I can wait for that kind of trouble."

"Good." Ariel was relieved. The two of them had made a pact not to wear makeup, although several of the girls in their class did. None of them wore as much as Dorrie Mae, though.

Robin smeared cleansing cream all over her face and began removing the cosmetics. She grimaced. "This stuff is hard to get off."

"Where did you get it, anyway?" Ariel idly inspected a tube of lipstick labeled Pale Pretty Peach.

"It's Pam's. She'd kill me if she knew."

"Where is she?" Robin's older sister was often at home on Saturday mornings.

"Sitting with the sugar babies."

Ariel groaned. She, too, had sat with the five-year-old Thomas twins. They were terrors. So she and Robin had renamed them.

"Anyway, I came over to ask you something," Ariel said. "Mother's going to take me to visit my father's late afternoon class next Monday. He's going to talk about France during the Middle Ages and especially about the cathedral at Chartres. That's where we're going. They think it will help me understand more about it. Do you want to come? It's after school. Then you can have dinner with us and we can do homework and you can spend the night. Ask your mom. OK?"

"I don't know anything about France in the Middle Ages," Robin said.

"I don't know much either. Maybe we'll learn something." Ariel loved to hear her father talk about the Middle Ages. It was his favorite topic and people said he was a world authority. Sometimes it seemed to Ariel that he knew more about more things than anyone in the world.

"OK," Robin said. "It sounds like fun."

So the following Monday Mrs. Marsden picked up the girls at school and drove them to the university. They sat in the back of the classroom. When Ariel's father came in he greeted them and then went to write on the blackboard.

He looked tall and slim in his gray suit. His curly hair became more and more tousled as he ran his fingers through it while he talked. It seemed to Ariel that it was as if he wanted to get closer to his brain with his fingers. His glasses were alternately on his nose or twirling in his hand. He frequently seemed about to drop them, but he never did.

Ariel was spellbound as her father made the past come alive that day. She could almost see the dancers as they entertained guests at a king's banquet. She could really hear the singers because her father played a recording of medieval songs. And on the slides her father showed she saw the great cathedral towering over the city.

After class they ate at a French restaurant near the university. "We'll be happy to share our *escargots* with you," her father said to the girls, his face solemn.

"What's that?" Robin asked.

"Snails." Ariel shuddered. "Poor little snails cooked in their shells."

"Yuck," Robin said.

But they enjoyed their crusty bread and the veal and baby carrots, shiny with butter. Dessert was pastry filled with whipped cream and covered with chocolate.

"I'll never eat again," Robin groaned on the way home.

"At least not until later tonight," Ariel's mother teased her.

At the Marsdens' the girls settled down to their homework in Ariel's room. After a while Robin asked, "Ariel?"

Ariel looked up. "What?"

"You know what Mr. Long said today about hydrogen bombs?"

Ariel shivered. "Sure I know. He said if a nuclear war starts, we could all be killed. Everybody. If it was bad enough, the whole world could be wiped out." She hated to think about it. She asked Robin, "Do you think it's true?"

"My brother thinks it's true and he's read a lot about it. He says that if a bomb landed on Los Angeles, a million people could be burned up right then. And everybody else a certain distance from LA would get sick from radiation and they'd die later."

"I don't believe it will happen," Ariel said. "If the generals and the President know what would happen, they wouldn't start that kind of a war. Neither would the Russians. Would they?"

"Ned says it could happen. There's an old man at our church who says it will. He says the Bible talks about it somewhere. The world is going to come to an end in fire, he says. He believes that God's going to make it happen when He gets mad at enough people."

Ariel stared at Robin in disbelief. Then she said, "That's not the kind of God my folks believe in. They say He's a God who cares about people. I know He wouldn't wipe everybody out."

"I hope your folks are right," Robin said. "Anyway, let's change the subject."

"You're the one who brought it up," Ariel reminded her friend.

"I know. Listen, I've been reading about the constellations. You know. For science. Come on outside with me, will you? I want to see if I can find my favorite. It's the Irish one."

"Irish? What are you talking about?" Ariel demanded.

"You know. O'Ryan." Robin giggled.

"Now who's being sick?" But Ariel had to laugh. "That's pretty good. Orion."

They went out to stand in the driveway. Although the night was dark, they could see only a few stars. The sky was faintly tinged with pink.

"What's that pink stuff?" Robin asked. "And why can't we see more stars?"

"It's smog," Ariel told her. "My father says we can't see the stars the way they really are because there's too much stuff in the atmosphere. He says we'd have to go way out in the country somewhere, away from any cities, to see the stars well."

"It's weird," Robin said. "Can you believe that the light we can see from those stars up there is thousands and thousands of years old? It takes forever to reach us."

"I know." Ariel thought about it for a moment. Then she asked her friend, "Have you ever wondered if anyone lives on the other planets out there? Or on the ones we can't see? I was disappointed when they found out nobody lives on Mars or Venus or Saturn. There's got to be somebody else out there. We can't be the only ones, can we?"

"I don't know." Robin sounded doubtful. "If there is life out there, why haven't some of the scientists figured it out? Why hasn't somebody been able to contact them? Or why can't they contact us? You know what I mean."

"I suppose it could happen," Ariel said.

"Sure it could." Robin sounded positive.

Ariel stared at the sky, trying to imagine another world like hers somewhere among the galaxies—

maybe a new world in which only good things happened. "I love to think about the stars," she said. "They're so mysterious. I wonder if anyone will ever know the answer."

"I wonder about it too," Robin said. "But maybe we'd better go back in. I've got to read some more."

"Me too." Ariel led the way back to her room and they began to work again. Soon, without realizing it, Ariel began to sing the song she had liked best from her father's lecture. It was lilting and happy, a dancing song. She didn't know the words, of course, since they were in old French. But she remembered the tune.

After a few moments Ariel's father stepped into the room. "Hello," he said to the girls. "How's it going?"

"Fine."

"You like that tune?" he asked Ariel.

"Yes. I like it best of the ones you played this afternoon."

"Had you heard it before somewhere?"

"No, I don't think so."

He nodded at her and smiled. "It's a good tune. You got it right."

Ariel could always remember a melody she liked, even after hearing it just once. Her friends and teachers made a big thing out of it, as if it were something special. But to her it was just the way it was, the way it had always been.

Now her father said, "Your mother says to come on out to the kitchen if you want a snack before you go to bed. It's about time for that. Are you finished with your homework?"

"Just about."

Robin and Ariel went to the kitchen where Ariel's parents sat together. "How about chocolate chip cookies and milk?" Ariel's mother asked.

"Why am I hungry after all that dinner?" Robin wondered.

"Because you're a bottomless pit, like Ariel," Mr. Marsden told her. Then he asked her, "What are you going to be doing this summer, Robin?"

"Nothing much. Mr. Marsden, are you sure Ariel couldn't stay with us? I'm going to miss her something awful."

"Oh, Daddy, please?" Ariel begged.

"I know you're going to miss each other. But I'm afraid it wouldn't work out. We need Ariel with us. It's nice of you to ask, though, Robin."

Ariel saw the look Robin gave her father when he wasn't watching. *Robin still misses her own father,* Ariel thought. *Even though he's been gone all this time.* Ned was her brother, not her father. Nothing could take the place of a father.

Ariel felt a rush of love for her own father, for her mother. Even if they did change her plans, she knew they loved her. And if something was wrong, she wanted to be with them. That was where she belonged.

4

Each day Ariel stood beside the great oak tree looking up at its branches, waiting, listening. It seemed to her that if she could hear it sing again, it would be a good omen. Perhaps they would not have to go away. Perhaps if the tree sang to her again, everything would be all right.

But she heard only the birds and the slight rustling of branches as the breeze touched them. She was sad much of the time, homesick before she ever left home. And, in some vague way, she was ashamed of herself.

Going to Europe was certainly an adventure and many girls would be excited about it. She knew that. Still, she could not think of anything except her own disappointment. She'd had to cancel her party and now she'd never know whether Kevin would have accepted her invitation.

Everything was dark and threatening where before life had been good. Ariel worried more and more about things she read in the papers and saw on TV news.

One evening at dinner she said to her parents, "The other day Mr. Long told us that the whole world could be destroyed by thermonuclear bombs. He said that if a bomb dropped on Los Angeles, everybody around would be killed. Robin and I have been talking about it. Her brother thinks it could happen. Is it true?"

Ariel's parents looked at each other. They were very

solemn. Her father answered her. "Yes. It's true. Unfortunately, it's true."

"But that's awful," Ariel protested. "Why would people want to use a thing like that?"

"Most people would not want to," her father said. "But the danger is always there, just because the bombs exist. And leaders have the power to make choices. Choices which would affect the entire human race."

"Do you think it will ever happen?" Ariel wanted her parents to assure her that something so terrible would never happen.

"We hope not."

"Mother?" Ariel turned to her mother, longing to hear her say *No*.

But her mother only said, "We must hope the world leaders will make sure that it never does happen."

"Did Mr. Long mention the summit meeting to be held in Geneva in September?" Ariel's father asked her. "Our President and the Soviet Secretary-General plan to meet to discuss important issues."

"Yes. But Mr. Long said that nobody really trusts anybody else, so that meeting may not accomplish anything. Isn't there anything kids can do about it?" Ariel asked. "Mr. Long said that the future may be in the hands of people like us. That's scary."

"The whole thing's scary," Ariel's father agreed. "It seems to me that right now young people like you and your friends could band together. 'Youth For Peace' or something like that. You could at least write letters to Congress Representatives, Senators, world leaders, and let them know how you feel. It would surely be worth a try."

The next time Ariel and Robin went to the Young People's Fellowship meeting at church Mr. Allison, the minister, greeted everyone and, as usual, asked them to sit in a circle. Kevin never came, but others of Ariel's friends were there. When they had all arrived they followed their usual procedure of joining hands for the opening prayer.

Ariel liked Mr. Allison. He seemed to understand all kinds of things; the personal problems of his young flock, tensions between teens and their parents, and world problems as well. He always used the same opening prayer. *May the words of our mouths and the meditations of our hearts be always acceptable in Thy sight, O Lord, our strength and our Redeemer.*

Ariel released Robin's hand and settled back. Mr. Allison looked around the group. His dark hair was tousled and a cowlick made a tuft stick straight up. But it didn't matter. His dark eyes were clear, his glance direct, and he made every person in the room feel valuable.

"So," he began, loosening his clerical collar as if it were too tight for comfort. "So, what's on your minds tonight?"

"Parents. What else?" People tended to laugh at Kim because he appeared to be a bumbling clown. Actually, he was at the top of his class and he was well-liked. His parents kept him on a tight leash, and Ariel was surprised that they permitted him to come to these meetings; even more surprised that they had been willing to let him come to her party. And now there wouldn't be a party.

"Are things any better at home?" Mr. Allison asked Kim.

"Well, they took off my handcuffs and let me come tonight." Kim rubbed his wrists in pretended pain. "Of course, I got all my homework done first."

Some of the others groaned. "Everything? Even physics?" Janice asked.

"Everything." Kim suddenly looked serious. "What I can't figure out is why my folks won't trust me. It's as if they are waiting for me to do something terrible just so they can pounce on me."

"Well, you've got to keep on fooling them," Mr. Allison said. "Don't let that terrible thing happen. We all know that you're a good person, and we all stand behind you. So don't give up."

How awful that would be, Ariel thought. *I'm really lucky. Even though I don't always understand them, my parents really do trust me. But . . .*

Mr. Allison looked around the circle. "Any other problems?"

Ariel wasn't sure whether she wanted to speak or not. She looked at Mr. Allison, trying to decide. He seemed to know that she was troubled. "Ariel," he asked, "is something bothering you?"

Ariel hesitated.

"Tell him," Robin whispered.

"Well," Ariel began, "something strange is happening at home. I had plans all made for my . . . well, I had plans made. And now my parents tell me that we're leaving right after school for England and France. They won't tell me why. It's all very mysterious, and I wish they'd tell me. Then it might be easier to leave."

Mr. Allison nodded. "I understand. My family and I are leaving rather suddenly, too, right after school. We are going . . . being sent . . . to Nicaragua. I know how you must feel. But I imagine there's a good reason, don't you? You have wise parents."

I wonder, Ariel thought. *I wonder if he's seen Mr. Herauld too. Could it be possible? I think he's trying to tell me.* Aloud she said, "Nicaragua's dangerous. Do you really have to go there?"

"Yes," Mr. Allison said. "I really have to. I was there before, you know, as a young man. I know the people and the language."

"Will you be gone long?" one of the boys asked. "We'll really miss you."

"I don't know how long we'll be gone. I'll miss all of you, too. Now, any other problems?"

Robin, who usually didn't say much, surprised Ariel by asking, "Mr. Allison, I want to know something. At school we've been talking about nuclear weapons. Mr. Long has told us what would happen to the earth if those bombs were exploded. He says it could mean the end of the world. Is that true?"

Ariel wondered if Mr. Allison would agree with the things her parents had told her. He was thoughtful and very grave when he answered Robin. "This is a serious thing," he began. "It may be the most serious threat mankind has ever faced. Does anyone know why I'm saying that?"

Kim said, "Because when God made the world He put human beings in charge of it. Everything was fine in the beginning. But people have messed it up. And now it looks as if we're about to blow it in a big way. If the United States and the Soviet Union keep on stockpiling thermonuclear weapons, somebody's going to use them, and that will be that."

"How could such a thing have happened?" Mr. Allison looked around the circle. "What has brought us so close to the brink?"

"Nobody trusts anybody." Andrea was a senior, and Ariel had admired her for a long time.

"Explain, please," Mr. Allison said.

"Well . . ." Andrea appeared to be thinking out loud. "The United States and the Soviet Union are both powerful nations. We are far apart in our ideologies, our moral standards; in our views toward human rights, for instance. We've been alienated from each other for so long that we seem to have forgotten how to talk, how to reason. I just can't believe that the Russians want an all-out nuclear war any more than we do. It would be crazy. There must be a way to resolve our differences without war. There *must* be."

Jack looked over at Andrea. "You're an idealist. It may already be too late. But I've got a question. What I want to know is, if God made the world and everything in it, why doesn't He stop this mad race? Doesn't he care about the earth? About us?"

"Ideas, anyone?" Mr. Allison asked.

"He cares, I think," Kim said. "But maybe He's fed up with us. I wouldn't blame Him. Maybe letting us use nuclear weapons would be a way He could zap us and start over."

"He wouldn't zap us," Andrea insisted. "We'd be zapping ourselves."

"Think back to our discussion of the qualities God has shown and still shows throughout history," Mr. Allison suggested. "What did we decide was the primary characteristic of God as we talked about it?"

Shyly Ariel said, "You called it *steadfast love*. You said that no matter what we do, God still loves us and cares about us and wants us to do better."

Luke, a senior, was planning to go to a theological seminary after graduation. Ariel thought he'd make a good minister. He was kind. Kinder than most of the boys she knew. "Ariel's right. And there's another thing."

"What's the text for this sermon, Luke?" Dan asked.

"Quiet," Jack said. "Let him talk."

Luke went on as if he had not been interrupted. "Jesus is called *The Prince of Peace*, not the general of an army. Somehow, sometime, He promised, His peaceable kingdom will be possible for all people. It may not look that way now, with all these awful things happening. But it's a promise, and I have to believe it."

The group was silent. After a while Andrea asked Mr. Allison, "I think Luke is right. But I don't see how it's going to happen. What if we blow up the world and it's all over? What can kids like us do to prevent it? I feel so helpless. The adults got us into this mess. We're only children, really. What can we do? Nobody will listen to us. We don't count."

"I hear the pain in your voice, Andrea," Mr. Allison said. "But I think you're wrong about something. Not everyone refuses to listen. Let's talk to the Eternal Listener now. Shall we join hands?"

So again hands were joined around the circle and it became very still. Mr. Allison said, "I believe we have been called together for a special purpose. Perhaps it was to put us in touch with God's power in a unique way here in this room at this moment. Let us pray together."

Breaking the moment of silence, Mr. Allison said, "Lord, Your children call upon You. We pray that You will be with us here at this moment, strengthening us, easing our pain, giving us wisdom. Be with Kim, Ariel, all of us who ask Your help."

After a long silence Andrea began to speak, faltering at first, but gaining strength. "Lord Jesus, You promised us peace. We aren't wise or grown-up, but You always said that people needed to be more like children, so maybe You'll listen to us. Please help us to help the world. We love it and we don't want it to be hurt any more than it already is. Amen."

One by one the young people added their prayers. After everyone had finished, Mr. Allison said, "Now don't forget. You can make a difference. Each one of you can make a difference. And may the Lord watch between us while we are absent, one from another." Ariel fought the lump in her throat. *He knows*, she thought. *I'm sure he knows.*

5

But in spite of herself, Ariel's thoughts were still focused mainly on her own problems.

In the days that followed, Ariel's parents began using French phrases, teaching her words and sentences she would be able to use in France. She thought the language sounded beautiful. Beautiful and strange. Sometimes words did not sound the way they looked on the page. *Chartres,* for instance. The city where they were going to live for a while.

"It is pronounced *Shart'ruh,*" her father explained. "The last *ruh* is touched very lightly at the end of the word, hardly sounded."

He had her try it over and over until she had it perfectly. He began calling her *Chèrie* instead of Darling. *Sheree,* he said, emphasizing those last two e's. She liked it.

One day her mother told her, "You need to be thinking about the things you want to take with you on the trip. Everything will have to fit into one suitcase and a flight bag. Take just the most important things. We want to travel light."

"I can tell you one thing I have to take," Ariel said. "Gladly. I'll never part with him."

Her mother smiled. "I know. But what else? Besides your clothes, I mean. And which clothes do you absolutely need?"

So Ariel made her lists and practiced packing her

two cases, trying to decide what to take and what to leave behind. She hated to leave any of her books. She decided on paperbacks since they took up the least room and weighed the least. Finally she decided to take *A Wrinkle in Time, The Arm of the Starfish, The Secret Garden, The Island of the Blue Dolphins,* and *A Bridge to Tarabithia*. She never grew tired of reading those books and she felt she couldn't live without them.

"*Chèrie,*" her father said, "there are books for sale in England and France, too, if you get desperate."

Ariel knew he was teasing her, but she didn't care. Her books were her most important possessions, next to Gladly.

***

The morning of the last day of school Ariel and Robin stood together in the schoolyard. Robin suddenly gasped and clutched Ariel's arm. "Look at that! I don't believe it."

Ariel looked at the boy entering the yard. It was Kevin, but it was a changed Kevin. Now his smooth brown hair was dyed a violent yellow and it stuck up in stiff tufts all over his head, as if it had been starched. A bright green streak had been painted down the middle of the center tuft. He wore a gold hoop earring in one ear.

Ariel could not believe what she was seeing. "What does he think he's doing?" she whispered to Robin. Others were pointing to him and laughing. A group of eighth-graders clustered around him, and Ariel thought they looked as if they were admiring him.

Robin laughed. "Does he think he's on TV?"

Ariel said, "It's ridiculous. I really hate it." Kevin was no longer the same boy who had carried her to the nurse's office, who had been kind and friendly. Now he looked like someone she didn't even want to know.

As they went back to the far side of the school ground Robin said, "Well, that should make it easier for you to leave him. Who'd want to be around someone who looks like that?"

"I wouldn't." Ariel felt a sense of relief. Robin was right. It would be easier to leave him.

On the way home from school that afternoon Robin asked Ariel, "Are you all packed?"

"No. That's what I'm going to do now. I left it till last because I wanted something to do when I get home. I know exactly how to do it. I've practiced a hundred times, I guess. Want to come and help me?"

Robin looked away. "I have to get ready for tonight. You know. Wash my hair and everything."

Ariel swallowed the lump which rose in her throat. "I hope you have a good time at the party. And don't forget to write to me at the hotel in Chartres."

"I won't. I've got the address. You'll write to me, too, won't you?"

"You know I will."

"Well," Robin seemed in a hurry to leave. "Well, so long."

"So long." Ariel watched her friend leave. She felt deserted, as if Robin had already stopped thinking about her. She hoped Robin might at least turn and wave. But she just walked away, without looking back.

Ariel went slowly toward home. She couldn't understand why Robin acted the way she did. Most of all she couldn't understand why her parents hadn't explained the reason for this trip. Here it was, the very day, and she still didn't know why they were going or what it was her parents were afraid of.

At home she found her mother sitting in the rocking

chair in her bedroom. Ariel saw that her suitcase was packed and closed, her flight bag standing beside it. Her mother just sat there staring at nothing.

"Mother?"

Emilie Marsden looked up. "Hello, honey. I didn't hear you come in." She spoke as if she had been faraway.

The pain in her mother's eyes startled Ariel. Once before she had seen that same expression. They had been looking at war photographs, pictures of burned Vietnamese children running, screaming in pain. Her mother had said, *I can't stand it when the children are hurt. When the innocent ones have to suffer.*

Ariel's father had said, *It's always the innocent who pay the greatest price.*

Now she ran to stand beside her mother. Without saying anything Emilie Marsden pulled her daughter down to her lap. She rocked Ariel as if she were a little girl again. They sat not talking, only being together.

Finally Ariel asked, "Is it because you feel sad about going away?"

"Partly that," her mother said.

"Well, if you feel so bad, why can't we just not go? Why can't we stay home?" She felt a moment of hope.

"I'm afraid it isn't that simple," Ariel's mother said. "It just isn't that simple." She sighed. Then she asked, "Do you want me to help you pack?"

"If you want to. Come and talk to me, anyway."

In Ariel's room her mother asked, "How was it at school today? The last day is always hard and this one must have been even harder for you."

"It was OK." Ariel didn't want to tell her mother about Robin just then, or about Kevin, either. Her mother felt bad enough as it was, and she did, too. So she just packed while her mother checked her lists for her.

At supper Ariel wasn't hungry even though cold

chicken and potato salad were among her favorite foods. "I guess I'm too excited to eat," she said. "I think I'll go get ready."

She went to her room to dress for the flight. She liked her new jeans. They weren't designer jeans, the kind Dorrie Mae wore, but they fit well. And she liked her new red and white striped top.

When she was dressed she looked in the mirror to comb her hair and quite suddenly she began to cry. She sat on her bed and held Gladly. Her tears made his fur wet, but she didn't care. She rocked back and forth with him as her mother had rocked her.

Soon her mother was beside her, her arm around Ariel's shoulder. "Oh, darling, I'm sorry. I'm so sorry."

Ariel leaned against her mother. "I don't want to go," she said between sobs. "And Robin was so funny when she said good-bye. She didn't want to come over or anything. She just said 'so long' and went home. She didn't even look back at me and wave. I waited. Maybe she doesn't like me anymore."

"You know that isn't true," her mother said. "She's your best friend, remember? Maybe she just doesn't like to say good-bye."

But Ariel was not comforted. She could only sob. Her mother stayed with her until at last she was able to control her tears. "You'd better go finish your stuff," she told her mother. "I'll be all right now."

When her father came to get her luggage, Ariel said in a rather shaky voice, "Hello, Daddy. I'm all packed."

He sat on the bed beside her, not saying anything, only holding her hand. She knew he was trying to help her. "I'm sorry you hurt so much," he said finally. "Sometimes life is pretty hard."

"Don't make me cry again, Daddy. I've just stopped and I don't want to start again."

Her father released her hand and kissed the top of her head. When he had left with her bags, Ariel looked around her room one last time. She had made her bed, but she smoothed it again. Books were tidy on the shelves. Her stuffed animals were neatly lined up, all but Gladly. Her window was locked. She whispered, "Good-bye," and went outside.

Once again she stood by the tree and looked and listened. Once again she heard only birds and rustling leaves. She was still listening and hoping when Robin's brother drove up in front of the house. Then she saw her. Robin got out of the car and came toward Ariel.

"Robin!"

"Hi." Robin wore the dress she'd chosen for the class party. Her shiny hair lay in soft waves around her face. She looked marvelous.

"What are you doing here?" Ariel still couldn't believe it. "Why aren't you at the party?"

"I'm going, but I have something for you. I wanted to surprise you. That's why I didn't say anything this afternoon."

"Oh, Robin." Ariel felt a great lifting. She opened the package. It contained a small leather coin purse with Ariel's name embossed on it in gold letters.

"It's beautiful," she told her friend. "I love it. Thank you. I'll think of you every time I use it."

"I'm glad you like it. Now have a good time and don't forget to write."

"You, too," Ariel said. "I wish you were coming with us."

"Oh, Robin, we wish you could come." Emilie Marsden leaned over to kiss Ariel's friend.

She's sad about leaving Robin, too, Ariel thought. *She still has that hurt look in her eyes.*

Robin got into the car and waved while Ned drove away. Ariel waved, too, until the car was out of sight. She felt almost happy. Her best friend did care about her, after all.

6

In spite of her reluctance about leaving home, Ariel
found that she was excited by the prospect of a flight
on the huge plane. She wondered how many people
were on board. Hundreds, surely. Ariel followed her
parents until they found their seats.

"We can take turns sitting together," her father said,
stepping out of the way of a man who carried hat, coat,
and briefcase. "Would you rather sit beside me or your
mother to start with?"

"I don't care. You choose," she told him.

"I choose myself, then. I'll even let you have the
window seat, although there won't be much to see, at
least for a while."

Then Ariel saw that her mother would be sitting
beside a young woman who was calmly reading. Ariel
suddenly made up her mind. If everything was going to
be strange on this trip, she might as well begin it by
sitting with a stranger.

"Daddy," she said, "I think you and Mother should
sit together. I'd like to sit here behind you, if that's all
right."

Her parents looked surprised, but before either of
them could speak, the young woman said to Ariel,
"Good. I'd like sitting beside you. And I'm very fond of
bears." She stood to make room. "Please take the window seat."

"Are you sure?" Ariel asked.

The woman nodded. Soon Ariel and Gladly were settled beside her. "Are you comfortable?" she asked Ariel with a friendly smile.

Ariel liked her face. Her glossy dark hair was smooth and her bangs accented eyebrows that tilted slightly. "Yes, thank you." Ariel fastened her seat belt and looked out the small window. In the glow of yellow lights she could see men in white jumpsuits scurrying about. She saw other planes taking off or landing. Everything was busy, almost festive. Her heart began to beat a little faster.

Soon she heard a man's voice on the loudspeaker. "This is your captain. We will be ready for takeoff shortly. Meanwhile the staff will acquaint you with the aircraft and our safety procedures. We hope you will have a pleasant flight."

Ariel watched the flight attendants demonstrate oxygen masks, emergency exits, and life rafts. "I hope we won't need any of those things," she said to her seatmate. She almost wished that she were sitting beside one of her parents.

"Don't worry." Her companion smiled at her. "Everything is going to be just fine."

Looking out the window, Ariel saw the men of the ground crew making hand signals. Soon she felt the plane begin to move, first slowly and then faster and faster down the runway.

"This is the part I don't like," she said. "I hate the way it feels and I hate the noise. I guess I'm silly, but I can't help it. I've flown before, but I still don't like this part."

The woman beside her took Ariel's hand. Before Ariel had much time to think, the plane was in the air and she watched the earth recede. Soon she could see only blurring paths of light, and then nothing.

Ariel's neighbor released her hand. In a moment

Hugh Marsden stood in the aisle looking down at them. "Everything all right?" he asked his daughter.

"I guess so. I don't like it just before he lifts the plane up. I don't like landings, either."

"I know how you feel," her father said. "I've felt that way myself." Then he spoke to the woman sitting by Ariel. "It was kind of you to give Ariel the window seat."

Emilie Marsden joined her husband and offered her hand to the stranger. "Our name is Marsden," she said.

The two women shook hands. "Mine is Foster. Julian Foster. Are you staying long in London?"

"Only a few days," Ariel's mother said. "Then we're going on to Durham."

"Durham. It's one of my favorite cities." Julian Foster smiled at Ariel. "I do hope you will like it."

Ariel's parents returned to their seats. For a few moments Ariel felt shy. She didn't know what to say. She didn't even know whether she should talk at all. Perhaps Julian preferred to be quiet.

But Julian looked at her and said thoughtfully, "Let's see if I can guess your age. I'd say about thirteen."

"You're close," Ariel told her. "I'll be thirteen in just a little while. July seventh. I was going to have a party, but it got canceled."

"I see. Well, a trip like this one can be even better than a party, can't it?"

"Maybe." Ariel was reluctant to admit that. As if to change the subject she asked, "How do you spell your name? I've never known anyone named Julian."

Julian spelled it for her. "Your own name is lovely," she said. "I've never known anyone called Ariel, so that makes us even."

"Where do you live?" Ariel asked her.

"In the city of Norwich." Julian pronounced it *Noritch.*

Ariel asked, "Do you like living there?"

"Yes, but I have nothing, no one to keep me there any longer."

Ariel thought Julian looked sad. She wondered what was wrong, but she didn't know how to ask so that Julian wouldn't think she was intruding.

As if Julian knew what Ariel was thinking she said, "I'm a nurse, you see. I had a patient in Norwich whom I tended for quite a long time. It became obvious that she would not recover and I was with her in her home for nearly a year."

"What happened?" Ariel asked.

Julian's blue eyes were clear; the look she gave Ariel was steady and deep. "She died peacefully. I was with her."

"How old was she?" Ariel asked.

"She died on her thirty-fifth birthday."

Ariel felt her heart beating in her chest. "My mother's thirty-five."

"Yes?" Julian's smile was reassuring. "She looks very healthy. I think you have nothing to worry about there."

"What was your patient's name?" Ariel asked.

"Her name was Ann."

"Do you miss her?"

Julian studied Ariel's face before she answered. Then she said, "Yes, I miss her, but I would not wish her back. Now I've had a holiday and I'm returning to England to look for a new position, perhaps in a different city. It will be rather like beginning a new life."

Like me, Ariel thought. Even with her parents in the seat ahead of her and with Julian, friendly and kind, beside her, she still felt unsettled, as if she were cut off from all the familiar things. But in spite of that, excitement bubbled up in her.

Again it was as if Julian sensed Ariel's thoughts

when she said, "A flight like this one always leads to some kind of an adventure, don't you think so?"

Ariel felt that she could trust this woman whom she didn't really know. "I guess so. But I don't even know why we're going on this trip. There's something secret about it and my parents haven't told me what it is. I can't help being worried."

"Don't you think they'll tell you when they can?"

"They say they will. I hope they will. Whatever it is, I think I'm old enough to know."

"I can understand how you feel," Julian said, "but don't you suppose your parents have their reasons?" Without waiting for an answer she asked Ariel, "Do you feel sleepy? It's getting rather late."

"No," Ariel told her. "I guess I'm too excited to sleep."

Julian took a book from her flight bag. "Well, don't you think that a good book takes one's mind off all kinds of troubles?"

"Oh yes." Ariel reached for the book in her own flight bag and showed it to Julian. "It's by my favorite writer. My parents gave it to me for this trip."

"*A Ring Of Endless Light.* How marvelous. I've read all her books, some of them more than once."

"What are you reading now?" Ariel glanced at Julian's book. It was *A Circle Of Quiet* by Madeleine L'Engle. They smiled at each other.

We even like the same writer, Ariel thought. She knew that she had found a new friend, even though they would be friends for only a short time.

That bothered Ariel. *These days nothing seems to last,* she thought. *Not even the things I could always count on, like being home. Like being with Robin. Is anything ever going to last?* Ariel sighed and opened her book.

7

The flight from Los Angeles to London did not seem long to Ariel. Everything was interesting: the bustle of people in the large cabin, the smiling, busy flight attendants, meals eaten at a little table which pulled down. And conversation with Julian.

"This is your first trip to England?" Julian asked Ariel.

"Yes. My parents have been there but I haven't."

"I understand that you will be only a few days in London," Julian said. "There's a great deal to see there. One needs a good deal of time."

"I hope we'll see Princess Di. Do you think we might?" Ariel couldn't help feeling hopeful about that.

"I wouldn't count on it," Julian said. "But there's always that chance."

From time to time Ariel dozed. She slept for a while when the movie was being shown and the cabin was darkened. And several times during the flight she changed seats with one of her parents.

"Mother," she said once, impatiently, "now can't you tell me what it is you and Daddy are so worried about? Why we had to leave home and come on this trip? I really want to know. I'd feel better about the whole thing if you'd tell me."

Her mother sighed. "I've told you before. As soon as we can, we'll tell you. Honestly we will."

"Well, I'm part of this family, too," Ariel said, "and I think I'm old enough to know, whatever it is."

But her mother did not tell her.

Shortly before the plane landed at Heathrow Airport in London Ariel asked Julian, "May I have your address? I'd like to write to you."

Julian looked thoughtful. "I'd enjoy hearing from you. We must keep in touch with each other. However, I won't have an address for a while because I'm not sure where I'll be. May I write to you somewhere?"

Ariel gave her the address of the hotel in Chartres where Robin was going to write to her. "Do you really think we'll meet again?" she asked Julian.

"I really do."

"I hope so." Ariel was disappointed when they became separated from Julian in the airport. She and her parents were caught up in the noise and activity in the vast building. Tired and confused, she could only think, *I wish I were home.*

***

The three days in London passed in a blur. Sometimes Ariel's father went out on errands so secret that he didn't explain them.

"Where does he go?" she asked her mother.

"I'm sorry. I can't tell you." Her mother sounded worried.

But at times the three of them explored London together. Even though she tried to pay attention to things her parents pointed out to her, Ariel felt as if she were only partly present. Her thoughts moved from these strange new sights to home and Robin, to Julian, and back again.

Westminster Abbey was simply a mass of people, as far as Ariel could see. And although they tried to watch the changing of the guard at Buckingham Palace, so many people crowded in front of her that Ariel saw nothing but the backs of other people.

Once, on a street corner, Ariel saw an old man clothed in a long white robe. He held a sign which he waved about as he cried in a shaky, weak voice, "Repent ye. The Day of Judgment is at hand. Repent and be saved."

As the Marsdens hurried past him, trying to catch a bus, Ariel looked back to see a group of boys tormenting the old man. She wished she could rush back to try to help him. The boys looked the way Kevin had, that last day of school.

Nothing felt right to Ariel, not all the time they were in London. Her parents were distracted, sometimes talking so softly to each other that she could not hear what they said. *It's that secret,* she thought angrily.

On the fourth day in London they rented a car and began the drive to Durham. From the back seat Ariel said, "Well, we didn't see Princess Di and I couldn't see the changing of the guard, and I don't like London very much. You said I would."

"I'm sorry," her father said. "We did rush you, didn't we?"

"Maybe you'll like Durham better," her mother said. "It's much smaller and there aren't such crowds of people. At least, there weren't when we were there. We loved Durham, didn't we, Hugh?"

Ariel remembered that her parents had gone to England on their wedding trip. They had stayed in Durham. She had heard them talk about the city and the cathedral.

Outside the car window green fields stretched for

miles, and groves of trees. Bands of sheep grazed; small stone farmhouses perched on hills or sat sturdily on flat land. Everything was so much greener than it was at home. Southern California was mostly brown in summer.

At last her mother said, "Look, Ariel. There's the cathedral and that's the castle, over to our left."

They drove along narrow, twisting streets, and Ariel caught sight of the two buildings. They stood near each other on a hill high above the city. Ariel thought they looked as if they had always been there.

Her mother turned to look at her. "How would you like to live in a castle for a few days?"

"Really?"

"Yes. We're going to have rooms there."

"Is it a real castle?" Ariel stared at the building as they drove toward it.

"It is." As Ariel's father stopped at the entrance to the castle grounds to talk to the gatekeeper, she heard the cathedral bells ringing. Suddenly she was wide awake, longing to get out of the car and begin to explore this place.

Ariel's father parked the car in the circular graveled lot which lay in front of the castle. Holding Gladly, Ariel got out and stretched. It had been a long ride and all her muscles were tight. She looked around her. Bending her head back she looked all the way up to the top of the castle and she saw it, round and strong against the wide sky. *I wonder which will be our room,* she thought.

Her father went toward the building marked *Office* and soon came out with a pleasant young woman who greeted Ariel and her mother.

"Hello. What do you think of our castle?" Her speech sounded like Julian's, crisp and clean. She picked up Ariel's suitcase and led the Marsdens to the entrance of the castle. "I hope you all have strong legs," she said. "Here come the stairs."

There were a great many of them and they were narrow, steep, and winding. Ariel held Gladly and struggled with her heavy flight bag. She felt sorry for her parents, each carrying two pieces of luggage. They seemed to climb for miles.

Finally they were in a long hall which was thickly carpeted and furnished with heavy tables and chairs. It was quiet there, and a bit gloomy. The young woman stopped before a large oak door. She unlocked it and opened it, and they all stepped into a beautiful big room.

"Who usually lives here?" Ariel asked, looking around her. "The Queen?"

Their guide smiled. "No. The university students live here during school term. It's holiday now and we let their rooms out to travelers like yourselves. Do you like this one?"

"It's gorgeous." Ariel was impressed. The room was furnished with a sofa, several chairs, some lamps, an ornately carved desk, and bookshelves crammed with books. The windows were covered with heavy red draperies. Ariel pushed them aside to look out. She looked straight across at the towers of the cathedral.

"Ariel," her mother called from the bedroom. "Which bed would you like?"

She looked into the spacious bedroom. Three single beds were arranged so that the room didn't appear crowded. One bed was beside a window. She went to look out. Then she stretched full length on the bed. Lying flat she could see the top of one of the cathedral towers. "May I have this one?" she asked.

Her father said, "It's yours."

"Where will we eat?" she asked.

"In the Great Hall at the other end of the castle and down all those stairs. I counted a hundred and thirty."

Her father groaned. "We'd better start now or we'll be late for dinner."

But there was time for a walk before dinner. They went out into the castle grounds. Orderly rows of flowers made bright spots against the castle walls. Ariel and her parents walked out the gates toward the cathedral.

They walked all around the cathedral on a path which led between thickly branching trees and bushes. At one point her father stopped and pointed down. "There it is," he said. "The River Wear."

Ariel looked down and saw the river far below. It was calm, flowing quietly between steep grassy banks. "I wish we could get a boat and ride on it," she said.

"We will. You'll love it." Her mother smiled at her husband. "We did, didn't we, Hugh?"

Her father put his arm around his wife. "We did, indeed. This is a special time for us," he told Ariel, "coming back here with you."

I'm glad I belong to this family, Ariel thought, *even though I do get mad at them sometimes.*

Soon they turned to go back to the castle. As they rounded a curve in the path, Ariel saw a man and a boy sitting on a bench. The boy looked very tired and pale. She thought he might be about her own age. His curly hair was cut short and lay close to his head, like a cap. His dark eyes had purple shadows beneath them. Another man stood talking with the two on the bench, his back to the Marsdens. Late sunshine touched the man's hair and he seemed to glow with light.

Then Ariel recognized him. "It's Mr. Herauld," she said, surprised.

"Hello, Ariel. I told you we'd meet again, didn't I?"

Her parents shook hands with him. Mr. Herauld introduced them to the other man and the boy. "This is Mr. Thomas Langley and his son, Aidan."

The boy rose slowly from the bench as everyone

started shaking hands. Ariel thought it looked as if it hurt him to stand.

"Are you staying at the castle?" Ariel's mother asked. "We're on our way over to dinner."

"Yes, we have rooms there," Mr. Langley told them. "Mr. Herauld, are you staying there, too?"

Mr. Herauld didn't answer the question. He only said, "Tomorrow we must talk."

Ariel looked at Mr. Herauld. *What are they going to talk about?* she wondered. *And when will they tell me what's going on?*

But when she looked at Mr. Herauld there was no answer for her in his eyes. Only the deepness she had seen before. And as she had shivered when she first saw it, so she shivered now.

8

The weather had changed during the night, and after breakfast Ariel and her parents walked over to the cathedral in a cool, soft rain which made everything smell fresh. The heavy doors were closed.

"Can you reach the door knocker?" her father asked her.

She looked up to see a bronze knocker on the wooden door. She could not decide whether it was shaped like the head of a lion or a demon. It looked fierce, with great empty staring eyes, a huge nose, and a mane of curling hair. In its open mouth was a burnished ring which could be lifted and lowered to clang against the spike upon which it rested. She reached to touch it. The ring felt smooth to her fingers.

Her father said, "Imagine for a moment that you are a man who lived over a thousand years ago and that you have been accused of a crime. You could run here to this building and knock with the knocker, even if it were the middle of the night. A monk who slept inside a cell up there, over the door, would let you in. For a while you could be safe here in the cathedral. No one could come after you because you would have sanctuary here."

"You mean in this very building?" Ariel laid her hand against the door.

"Yes. This door knocker is an exact copy of the original one. The real one is inside in the Treasury Room. You can see it and touch it later. Let's go inside now."

The Marsdens stepped inside the cathedral. The first thing that struck Ariel was its size. It was enormous. The arches were rounded, the tops of some of them carved with intricate designs. The pillars were thick and massive, and many of them were carved in differing patterns. Ariel thought she had never seen such a strong building. One would certainly be safe here, she believed, no matter what happened.

Then Ariel saw a man walking toward them down a side aisle. He was robed in a gray garment which fell to the floor. Ariel could see that the garment had a hood. He walked slowly, his eyes lowered.

Ariel thought she might be seeing a ghost. Her father had said that monks lived here long ago. "Is he real?" she whispered. "Is he a real monk?"

"Yes," her father answered softly. "He is one of the reasons we are here."

The monk stopped in front of the three of them. He looked at Ariel first. He looked at her for quite a long time, studying her face as if he wanted to memorize it. She returned his look. She wanted to look at him forever, but she knew it was impolite to stare. Then he smiled at her and she smiled, too.

I love him, she thought. *I don't even know him, but I love him.*

Ariel's father said, "Brother Michael?"

The monk nodded calmly.

"May I please introduce myself and my family? I am Hugh Marsden from California. This is my wife, Emilie, and our daughter, Ariel."

The monk shook hands with Ariel's parents. He laid his hand against Ariel's cheek for a moment.

Then Ariel saw Mr. Langley and Aidan walking down the aisle toward her father and the gray monk. "Look, Mother," she whispered. "Here come Aidan and his father. Aidan looks sick, doesn't he? I wonder what's wrong with him."

"You're right. He doesn't look well." Her mother sounded concerned. "But he must be well enough to be here with his father. Do you think the two of you could look around the cathedral together for a while this morning? We adults have to meet with Brother Michael and Mr. Herauld. You and Aidan will be perfectly safe here, and we'll meet for lunch in the Great Hall."

Ariel felt shy. "What if he doesn't want to talk to me? I don't know what to say to him."

"I imagine you'll find plenty to talk about," her mother said.

When the adults went off leaving Ariel and Aidan together they stood silently for a few uneasy moments. Then, as if on a signal, they said at exactly the same time, "How do you like Durham?"

They laughed and it was easier after that. Ariel asked, "What do you want to look at first? Anything special?"

"Yes. Come on. I'll show you."

Aidan led her to a spot behind the high altar at the far end of the building. Up a few steps they saw a floor of rough stone and in the middle of that floor a large gray stone slab flanked by four candleholders, each one higher than a man, and each holding a candle that was taller than a man.

"What is it?" Ariel whispered.

Aidan's voice was soft when he answered. "It's the tomb of St. Cuthbert. His bones are buried under there. They said long ago that if someone who was sick came here to pray, St. Cuthbert would help heal him." Suddenly he asked, "Do you care if we sit down for a while?"

Ariel looked at him. All the color had drained from his face and she could see perspiration on his forehead.

"Sure. Let's find some chairs. Are you OK?" She felt sure that he was not.

"I'll be all right. I just need to sit down."

They went back into the nave and sat together. Ariel didn't know whether Aidan wanted to talk about himself, and she didn't want to pry. But she wanted to know more about him. She asked, "How old are you?"

"Twelve. How about you?"

Ariel thought that Aidan was having trouble catching his breath, but she didn't say anything about it. "I'll be thirteen pretty soon. Our names are something alike, aren't they?" she said. "Ariel and Aidan. They both start with *A* and they both have five letters."

"And they're both unusual," Aidan agreed. "What does yours mean? Do you know?"

"The Lion of God. But I don't feel much like a lion. There's an Ariel in a play by Shakespeare, too, my parents say."

"Yes. *The Tempest*. Ariel's a good name. I like it. Do you?"

"I've always liked my name. What does Aidan mean?"

"It means Fire."

She asked him, "Where do you live?"

"In Ohio. My father teaches art history at a university."

"Mine teaches in a university, too, in California. Medieval history." Ariel already liked this boy who looked so thin and tired. She felt, in a strange way, that they had known each other for a long time. "I want to ask you something," she said, making up her mind.

Aidan nodded. "What?"

In a rush she asked, "Do you know anything about why we're all here in Durham? Something really weird is going on. I'm sure something's wrong and my parents won't tell me what it is. Do you understand any of it?"

"Not really. I know something important is happening. My father is worried, too. Of course he always worries about me, but this is something new. He hasn't told me what it's about. He just says he'll tell me when he can."

Ariel was relieved to be able to talk to someone who felt the way she did. "It's really hard to wait, isn't it?"

"Yes. But I guess we have to." He paused a moment before he said, "Mr. Herauld. There's something odd about him."

"I know." Ariel did not plan what she said next. She just said it. "I had a dream about him the night before he came to our house."

Aidan stared at her. Then he said, "So did I. He came on the second of June. I dreamed about him . . . about our house the night before. I'm almost afraid to think about what that means."

"Me too."

Aidan was beginning to look a little better. The perspiration was gone from his forehead and his breathing was more relaxed, although he was still pale. But he had been pale yesterday, too.

All at once Ariel felt that she had to know. "Listen," she said. "Please tell me. Are you sick?"

When he answered it was as if he had trouble getting the words out. "You might as well know. Yes, I'm sick. They haven't told me for sure, but I think they know I'm not going to get well. I'm going to die. I don't talk to my father about it because it makes him so upset and sad." He paused before he said, "I've never told anyone else."

Ariel couldn't speak. Her mouth was dry and her heart began to pound so that she could hear it inside her ears. She stared at Aidan. Then she said, "But you can't die. You're only twelve. Like me."

"I know."

"Maybe they're wrong." Ariel desperately wanted

them to be wrong, whoever *they* were. The ones who had said he might die.

"Maybe. But the doctors all say the same thing. So I guess they aren't wrong."

"What about your mother? Where's she?"

"I never knew her. She died when I was born. It's always been my father and me. He'll be really lonely when . . . if . . ." He stopped abruptly. Then he said, "Let's not talk about it anymore right now. OK?"

"But," Ariel insisted, "just tell me what it is. What do they think is wrong with you?"

"They haven't told me exactly. I guess they aren't sure themselves. But it's something pretty basic. My heart and my blood. I've had all kinds of tests and treatment, but they haven't found a cure yet for whatever it is that's wrong with me."

Ariel didn't know what to say.

"The doctors didn't want me to come on this trip," Aidan told her. "They'd like me to be in the hospital. But my father and I and Mr. Herauld decided I should come anyway." He stood then, steadying himself against a chair. "Come on. Let's walk around some more. I like this place. It makes me feel sort of safe."

Ariel knew what he meant. It did feel safe. As if no matter what went on outside, one could be protected here in this sheltering old building. But Aidan, her new friend, with no mother? Aidan, so sick that he might die. Would he be safe anywhere?

9

"We've studied the tide charts," Ariel's father told Mr. Langley the next night at dinner. "Tomorrow would be a good day to visit Lindisfarne. Would you and Aidan like to go with us? We'll leave right after breakfast and be back in time for dinner."

"That's kind of you." Mr. Langley considered it. "I can't go, I'm afraid, but I believe Aidan would enjoy the trip."

"What's Lindisfarne?" Ariel asked.

"It's an island in the North Sea," her father explained. "A group of monks first went there in the middle of the seventh century. For a while St. Cuthbert was their bishop."

Aidan asked quickly, "The same Cuthbert whose tomb is in the cathedral here?"

"Yes," Thomas Langley said. "And the other man whose tomb is here is St. Bede."

"I'd like to go," Aidan said.

"That's fine then. But you'll remember to be careful, won't you?" Mr. Langley sounded worried.

"We'll take good care of him," Emilie Marsden assured Aidan's father.

So the next morning they drove toward Lindisfarne. "I'm glad the sun's shining," Ariel said to Aidan.

He nodded, but he was very quiet.

"How about singing some rounds?" Ariel's mother asked after a while, breaking the silence.

They sang three-part rounds, Ariel against Aidan against Mr. and Mrs. Marsden. They sang "Row Your Boat" and "Scotland's Burning" and "White Coral Bells."

"Your voice is really pretty," Aidan told Ariel.

"Thanks. I love to sing."

"We're almost there," Ariel's father said finally. "We're coming into Lindisfarne."

Ariel looked at the cement road which stretched ahead of them. "I thought it was an island. I thought we'd go in a boat." She was disappointed.

"It is an island," her father said, "and people used to have to come and go by boat. But this causeway was built so that it would be easier to get here."

Once again Ariel was disappointed as they entered the village and drove down an ordinary street past old houses, stores, and inns. "I thought it would be different," she said.

"Wait until you see the priory ruins," her father said. "You'll forget about this."

He parked the car. They took their jackets and lunch boxes and walked toward the ruins. They paused for a moment to look at a stone cross, high as a man, which stood under the branches of a large tree. Ariel noticed that it was the usual kind of cross except that the upper part of this one rested against a stone circle.

"That's a Celtic cross," Aidan said. "There's one like it in front of the cathedral at Durham."

They walked toward the ruins. As if the four of them had the same thought at the same time, they all stopped to stare.

The wind was cold, the sky so blue that Ariel thought she might be able to touch it if she could reach high enough. The buildings were only shells, empty and gaping, covered with climbing vines. But the high pillars were sturdy and the rounded arches looked strong, although there was no roof to support them. Ariel looked at the sea and shivered.

"Cold?" Her father put his hands on her shoulders as he stood behind her.

"Yes. It's the wind, I guess." She pulled up the hood of her jacket. "Are you cold?" she asked Aidan.

"I'm OK." He pulled up his own hood. The wind blew color into his face and Ariel thought he looked almost healthy. "I don't know why exactly," Aidan said, "but I really like this place. Can we stay here a while?"

"As long as we like," Hugh Marsden told him. "We're not due back in Durham until dinnertime."

"What did the monks do here?" Ariel asked her father.

"What monks always do. They lived a life of prayer and good works. They supported themselves on this small island."

Aidan asked, "Why are the buildings ruined? When did it happen?"

"It happened gradually, over hundreds of years," Hugh Marsden explained. "These buildings were not the original ones. These come from medieval times. They became ruins because they were out of use for so long."

"I still like it here," Aidan said.

"I do too." Ariel looked around her. "It's a special kind of place. But didn't the monks get cold?"

"I'm sure they did," her father said. "But I imagine they didn't think much about their own comfort."

"Nobody lives like that anymore, do they?" she asked her father.

"Oh yes, but we don't hear much about it."

Aidan said, "We mostly hear about the bad things that people do to each other, don't we? Like murders and all the terrorists. And the nuclear bombs."

Hugh Marsden looked grim. "I'm afraid that's true."

Emilie Marsden glanced at her husband. Quickly she

asked, "Is anyone hungry? We could find a spot and have lunch."

They sat on the grass in the shelter of a ruined building. Ariel leaned against an ancient pillar, huddling against the wind. She looked at the sea. Wind made whitecaps on the water; gulls soared, wild and free. She shivered again. But it was not only because she was cold. Something about this spot was so unusual, so powerful, that she felt almost as if she had moved back, far back into another time.

When they had finished their lunch they wandered among the ruins. Ariel's mother paused from time to time to sketch.

"I'd like to be able to catch the true feeling here," she said, "but it's elusive. Can you imagine how magnificent these buildings must have been, rising against that marvelous wide sky, so near the sea?"

Finally they went back toward the Celtic cross which marked the entrance to the grounds. They stood under the tree while Emilie Marsden sketched the cross.

And then Ariel heard it. Standing near the ancient cross, leaning into the cold wind, Ariel heard the tree begin to sing. It was the same voice she had heard in the oak tree at home, the voice she had not heard for so long.

As she looked up into the tree she felt that she could see its very heart. The leaves began to shine, each with a life of its own, until the entire tree was alive, burning, trembling with song.

Then she realized that Aidan was staring up into the tree. She could see that he was listening to something. Did he hear the singing? Was it possible that someone else heard it, too?

Their eyes met, and then she knew for sure.

10

"Ariel?" Her mother had been speaking to her and she had not heard. The magic moment ended. The tree was silent. "You both look tired and cold," she said to Ariel and Aidan. "Would you like some hot chocolate? We can find a tea shop and rest for a while and get warmed up. You might like to buy some postcards, too."

They stopped in a crowded little shop to buy cards. Ariel selected some showing the ruins of the priory. She paid for them with coins from the new purse with her name on it. *I'll write to Robin,* she thought.

Aidan bought cards, too. From time to time they looked at each other, but they did not speak. Then the four of them strolled up the main street of the island village until they found a tea shop which looked cozy and very old. A sign in the window said *Tea and Scones.* A gray kitten slept beside the sign in a puddle of sunlight near a pot of scarlet geraniums.

Ariel and Aidan drank hot chocolate. Hugh Marsden studied his map. Ariel's mother worked on the sketch of the Celtic cross while she sipped her tea.

Ariel looked at the sketch. "Put the tree in, too. The big one above the cross."

Emilie Marsden nodded and continued drawing. Ariel and Aidan glanced at each other and then looked down again. It was as if they hesitated to communicate about the singing tree, even with a look.

Ariel chose a postcard for Robin. It showed part of

the monastery and the sea. She wrote, *We were here today. It's a very interesting place.* But when she had written it she knew that none of her true feelings about Lindisfarne showed. Robin wouldn't know how she really felt.

When they got into the car for the ride back, Ariel saw that Aidan was very pale again. "Tired?" she asked him.

"A little."

"So am I," she said.

Emilie Marsden turned to look at them. "Why don't you sleep a while? It would be good for both of you."

Ariel tucked Gladly under her cheek like a pillow, leaned against him, and closed her eyes. She slept deeply. In her sleep it seemed that she could hear the tree singing, or that she heard the calling of the white gulls high above her. She would waken with a start to find Aidan asleep beside her and no tree, no gulls. Then she would sleep again.

"Ariel. Aidan. Can you wake up?"

Ariel roused at the sound of her mother's voice. She felt hot and drowsy. Aidan sat up and looked around as if he didn't know where he was. Then Ariel saw the castle. "We're home," she said. "There's Brother Michael."

The monk came walking toward them. Ariel and Aidan got out of the car to greet him. "Have you had an interesting day?" he asked.

"Oh yes," Ariel told him. "We went to Lindisfarne."

"Lindisfarne." The monk echoed the word as if it were precious. "And you, Aidan. What did you think of Lindisfarne?"

"I want to go back. I hope I can." Then, without any warning, Aidan appeared to fold in upon himself and he slipped to the ground. Ariel watched in horror as blood flowed from his nose. He lay with his eyes closed, without moving, and his face grew whiter and whiter.

Hugh Marsden knelt beside Aidan and lifted his head. Brother Michael disappeared and returned almost immediately with Aidan's father and with a woman who carried a basin of water and some cloths.

"That's right," the woman said. "Let's just get this bleeding stopped. We'll have him fine in no time at all." She sounded matter-of-fact, as if she were positive that Aidan would be all right.

Ariel turned away and leaned against her mother. She didn't want to watch. Aidan's father knelt beside him on the ground.

Soon Brother Michael said to the woman who was helping, "That's better. Thank you, Marian."

Mr. Langley thanked her, too, and then he spoke to Aidan, who opened his eyes and looked about him, dazed. "Well, Aidan. You're with us again. You've had a bit of a nosebleed. Just rest here for a moment or two until you feel better."

"I'm sorry," Aidan said weakly.

"You couldn't help it," Ariel protested.

The woman tilted Aidan's head until she was sure the bleeding had stopped. "That's better," she said. "Good as new." Then she wiped Aidan's face with a damp cloth. She nodded cheerfully and left.

"We'll get you to bed for a while," Aidan's father said. "I'll carry you up."

"No, I can walk," Aidan insisted. But he walked very slowly. He turned to say to Ariel, "I'm OK. Really. This has happened before. I always get over it."

"Of course you do," Aidan's father agreed. "But just now rest is what you need."

"I'll see you tomorrow," Aidan told Ariel as he left with his father.

Ariel watched them go. She couldn't forget Aidan's face as it had looked, so still and white. Hugh Marsden reached out and laid his hand against his daughter's cheek for just a moment. She touched her father's hand, comforted by its familiar warmth and strength.

11

"We could pretend that the whole world is as peaceful as it is here," Ariel said to Aidan. They sat together in a sightseeing motorboat steered by a long-haired young man who chewed on a toothpick as he sat, relaxed and easy, at the wheel. He seemed to enjoy what he was doing.

"Hi there, kids," he had said when he took their money. "Where you from? Americur?"

"How did you know?" Ariel was surprised.

"Heard you talk, di'n't I? Nice place, Americur? Always wanted to go there myself. See Hollywood and all them movie and telly stars. Climb aboard. Maybe we'll go partway there today. Right?"

They had laughed because he was so cheerful and good-natured. A few other people were aboard the small boat. A grandmother and her two small grandchildren sat far forward, the children pointing out each dragonfly, each water bird.

"Look at the ducks, Gran!" the little boy called. "Four of them."

"That's a paddlin' of ducks," their friendly motorman said. "If they was flyin', they'd be a baldin' of ducks. If they was geese, they'd be a skein of geese. Know what they'd be if they was owls?"

"What?"

"A parliament of owls."

"Tell us more," the little girl begged.

In a kind of singsong the young man recited, "A kindle of kittens, a leap of leopards, a murder of crows."

"How do you know all that?" Ariel asked him.

"Us English is wise folk." He made a long, solemn face and everyone laughed.

"Really, Aidan," Ariel said, "let's do pretend that the other world doesn't exist. I love it here."

"My imagination isn't that good." Aidan's tone was wistful. "Haven't you been reading the newspapers?"

Ariel admitted that she had not. "And I'm glad we don't have television in the castle. I don't want to watch the news. I don't want to know about murders and muggings and what the Russians are doing. I want to pretend that everything's peaceful. Like it is right here."

Aidan sounded impatient and angry. "You can't be an ostrich and stick your head in the sand. You have to realize what's going on out there. Terrible things happen every day. Every hour. I feel so helpless. Sometimes I think I'd get well if all those things weren't happening."

"You really are right," Ariel agreed. "And I've been wondering if there isn't something kids like us could do."

"What?" Aidan asked. "Nobody listens to children." He sounded hopeless.

Ariel thought of the Young People's group at home, and the things Mr. Allison had said. *Somebody listens, Aidan,* she thought. But she didn't say anything out loud. Maybe later, when she knew her new friend better.

During the days they had spent in Durham, Ariel had watched Aidan grow more and more silent, more tired, more pale. She was sure his body hurt him sometimes because he walked carefully, as if he didn't want to jar himself. But at other times he seemed almost well. He never mentioned his pain or the episode in the parking lot. Now she realized that he must think about his illness more than he talked about it.

The breeze from the river felt cool against her face, and she watched the sun sparkle on the water. She listened to the two young children laugh with excitement as another boat passed them, making small waves which rocked the motorboat.

On shore again they climbed the steep path up to the road."Want an ice-cream cone?" Aidan asked her.

"Sure. I hope they have chocolate."

They strolled back toward the cathedral, eating their ice cream, watching the people. Two boys passed them, each with hair like Kevin's, dyed and streaked with green and standing up stiffly. They wore sleeveless black leather vests. One of the boys winked at Ariel. She didn't like the way that wink made her feel. Uneasy. Almost frightened.

Twice on the short walk Aidan stopped to rest, once leaning against a tree and once sitting on a bench just at the edge of the cathedral grounds. Sunlight fell on a patch of scarlet geraniums, making them glow as if they were on fire. A white cat sunned itself in the grass near the flowers.

"It reminds me of Lindisfarne," Aidan said.

Ariel nodded. "Yes, I remember." Then she asked him, "Are you OK now?" She didn't know how much to say to Aidan. She didn't want him to think she was too curious.

"I'm fine. I just get tired and out of breath. I don't have enough red corpuscles and my heart doesn't always pump right. But the river ride was nice and I feel better now. Let's go."

They went into the Galilee Chapel where St. Bede's tomb stood. Four large candleholders flanked it, and an arrangement of yellow lilies, white daisies, and tall field grasses stood in the large pottery jar near a corner of the tomb.

"Why don't you sing something?" Aidan asked. "There's nobody else here. I'd like to hear you sing again."

"I'm not sure I should. Do you think anyone would care?"

"No. Please sing something."

Ariel thought for a moment. Then she said, "All right. But I hope nobody comes in."

"It won't matter," Aidan assured her. "Just sing."

So Ariel sang an old French folk song which her father had taught her.

When she had finished singing, Aidan sat for so long without moving that she wondered if he had fallen asleep. But he said, "That was wonderful. Thanks."

She smiled. "You're welcome. Now would you like to go to the Treasury Room?"

He nodded. They had spent a good deal of time in that room, looking at the marvelous things which were displayed there. They touched the sanctuary knocker each time they looked at it. It was worn and smooth from the touch of many hands. Ariel liked to look at St. Cuthbert's cross, the one he had worn around his neck. It was small, made of gold and inlaid with garnets.

Now they stood before the locked glass case looking down at the cross which was protected from air and people. Ariel said, "I wonder who made it."

"I don't know. One of the monks, maybe. Whoever did lived over a thousand years ago. The cross was buried with St. Cuthbert. They found it when they opened his coffin."

They stood looking at the cross for a long time. Finally Aidan said, "I wish I could touch it."

"Why?" Ariel thought she knew.

But Aidan only said, "No special reason. I'd just like to touch it."

As they stood there, the dean of the cathedral came to the display case, a key in his hand. "Good morning," he said. "How are you both today?"

"We're fine, sir."

Ariel thought that Aidan didn't look fine, but he said so anyway.

"I'm taking our greatest treasure out to have its picture taken. The photographer is waiting for me." He unlocked the case and carefully took the cross into his hand. It looked even smaller, lying in the large hand of the dean. He looked at Aidan. "How would you like to hold it a moment?"

Aidan only stared up at the tall clergyman.

"He'd like to," Ariel said quickly.

Aidan held out his hand, palm up. The dean placed the cross on Aidan's palm. He looked at it silently. It seemed to Ariel that he stopped breathing. Then he looked at Ariel, his eyes full of wonder.

The dean picked up the cross again and turned to her. She held out her hand and he laid the cross in it. Ariel looked at it lying there, small and beautiful, the garnets glowing like little flames. Her whole hand tingled. Nobody spoke when the dean took the cross and walked away. He nodded and smiled at the children as he left.

Together Ariel and Aidan went into the cathedral. Silently they walked down the long side aisle, up the few steps behind the high altar, and straight to the tomb of St. Cuthbert.

Ariel prayed silently. *Lord, You have healed people; won't You please heal Aidan?*

While they stood there together by the great stone slab, Brother Michael joined them. "I rather thought I might find you here," he said. "The dean told me that each of you held St. Cuthbert's cross."

"Oh, Brother Michael," Ariel said, "I'll never forget it. My whole hand tingled."

"I am not surprised. I held it once myself, and I know exactly what you mean." He turned to Aidan. "And you. Did your hand tingle?"

Aidan started to speak, but he began to tremble. Ariel could see his body shake. The monk knelt so that his face was level with Aidan's. He put his hands on the boy's shoulders. "What is it? Can you tell me, Aidan?"

"I'm going to die," Aidan cried, "and I'm afraid. I thought if I held St. Cuthbert's cross, he might make me well. He's supposed to be able to work miracles, isn't he? But I don't feel any different. I'll never be well."

Brother Michael gathered Aidan into his arms and held him close. Then he said to the children, "Let us make a small circle here, the three of us, and stand together for a moment."

They joined hands. As they stood there, not speaking, Ariel felt a strange, mysterious power all around her, and the same kind of tingling she had felt when she held the golden cross. *Something good is happening,* she thought. *I don't know what it is, but I believe it.*

Aidan sighed deeply. He looked surprised as he said, "I don't feel afraid anymore."

Brother Michael nodded without speaking.

"I'm not afraid," Aidan said again.

Ariel knew it was true. But a sadness deeper than any she had ever known touched her like a cold wind from the North Sea.

12

That afternoon Ariel went with her parents for a long drive into the country. All the while she thought of Aidan and of the things Brother Michael had said. She wondered what it would be like to be as sick as Aidan was, so sick that he had to think about dying.

Her mother turned to look at her. "You're very quiet this afternoon. Are you all right?"

"Yes." Ariel didn't feel like talking just then, even though there were many things she wanted to ask her parents. She stared out the car window at the countryside. Everything was green and fresh. A sudden shower of rain fell, making the grass smell sweet.

"Ariel, look over to our right." Her father sounded pleased. Ariel turned to see a rainbow arch across the sky, its colors shimmering in the distance. *I'd like to touch it,* she thought. *I'd like to take some of it to Aidan.*

They stopped for tea in a small village. A friendly woman led them to a table in a rose garden. Tall hollyhocks lined the garden walls, and small yellow flowers which Ariel couldn't name were scattered among marigolds and pansies. Their table was covered with a blue and white cloth. Butterflies dipped into blossoms, bees hummed, and the air smelled of roses.

While her parents drank their tea Ariel sipped lemonade. The scones were hot, buttery, and plump with currants. But Ariel wasn't very hungry. She watched her mother sketch the hollyhocks which lined the walls.

At last her father asked her, "What's bothering you? Can't you tell us?"

She didn't stop to think about her answer. It just came. "Daddy, do you ever think about dying?"

Her mother looked up from her sketch. Her father said, "Yes. I believe we all think about it sometimes. Why are you asking me now?"

Ariel didn't answer him. She asked her mother, "Do you think about it, too?"

"Sometimes. Not all the time, though. Why?"

"Aidan thinks he's going to die." She wanted her mother to say, *Of course he isn't going to die.* But she didn't say anything. Ariel was frightened. "You think he's right, don't you?"

"We hope not," her mother said, "but he is very sick."

"Why do things like that happen?" Ariel cried. "Aidan's only twelve, like me. It isn't fair."

Her mother's voice was troubled. "Of course it isn't fair. Even the wisest people in the world have never been able to understand things like this. Sometimes things happen that none of us can explain."

"But they're such terrible things," Ariel said. "People kill each other. People die in accidents. Kids like Aidan get sick and die. And the whole world could end if somebody uses those awful bombs."

"You have to try to understand something," her father said. "People make choices, and the bad things that happen are often the result of those choices."

"Aidan didn't choose to be sick," Ariel protested.

"Of course he didn't," her father agreed. "But sometimes people do choose to do evil, harmful things. Then everyone suffers."

Suddenly Ariel remembered what Aidan had said.

Sometimes I think I'd get well if all those things weren't happening.

Everything's wrong, she thought. Her anxiety about Aidan grew and deepened.

***

Aidan and Mr. Langley were not in the dining hall for dinner. Somehow Ariel was not surprised. After the meal she and her parents went for a walk, strolling around the cathedral, looking down at the river, and then walking back to the castle. Ariel read for a while in her bed by the window. *A Ring of Endless Light is about dying,* she thought, looking up from the book, *but it doesn't make me sad. I wish I could be more like the people in that book.*

When she finally went to sleep that night with the sound of the cathedral bells in her ears, she dreamed that she saw a young boy standing at the edge of the sea, looking across the water. She heard him begin to sing. She tried to hear the words, but she could only hear the melody.

She wakened suddenly, and awake she still heard the singing. She glanced at her parents. They slept deeply in their separate beds. She sat up in her own bed and looked out. Although there was neither wind nor moonlight, Ariel saw a large plane tree glowing with light which came from the tree itself. The glistening leaves and branches bent and swayed. The tree seemed to be alive. Then she knew where the song came from.

Almost forgetting to breathe, she listened to the music, sweeter than any she had ever heard—even sweeter than the tree at home or the tree on Lindisfarne. *If only I could understand the words,* she thought. *If only I knew what it was singing about. I wonder if Aidan hears it, too.*

Then she heard a knocking at the outer door. She awoke her parents. "Someone's knocking," she whispered.

Her mother and father put on their robes, and her father opened the door. It was Brother Michael. "May I speak to Ariel, please?" she heard him ask softly. She put on her robe and went to join her parents.

"Ariel," the monk's tone was gentle, "please do not be afraid. Aidan is asking for you. Will you all come with me now?"

Ariel took her mother's hand and they followed Brother Michael along twisting corridors, up stairs and down again until they came to another part of the castle. A door was open. Mr. Langley stood looking into a bedroom. Ariel thought he was like a statue standing there, motionless and silent.

The monk took Ariel's hand. "Remember, you must not be afraid."

"I'll try not to be." Ariel clutched his hand and together they went into the room where Aidan lay. A stranger stood at the other side of the bed, his fingers on Aidan's wrist.

Aidan's eyes were closed. He was very still. All the color had left his face. She saw that his chest was rising and falling slowly. He opened his eyes and looked at her.

"How do you feel?" she asked him.

"I feel wonderful," he whispered. "I feel so light. And I don't hurt anyplace. I know I'm going to be all right. I want to tell you something." He spoke slowly, as if it were an effort. "About the trees. Did you hear the one just now?"

"Yes." Ariel was glad that he had heard it, too. "First

I dreamed I heard singing. Then I woke up and it was the tree."

Aidan was looking at her, but it seemed hard for him to hold his eyes open. He began to speak again, but his voice was so weak that Ariel could hardly hear what he said. She leaned forward to catch the words.

"The singing," he said. "I know why now."

"What, Aidan?" she asked. "What do you know?"

"I know . . ." Aidan's eyes widened, and a great shining smile lit his face. He took a deep breath.

Ariel watched him, waiting for his answer, but he didn't speak. She glanced up and saw the doctor turn to Mr. Langley with a long, quiet look.

Brother Michael stepped forward. Gently he closed Aidan's eyes, and he and Aidan's father knelt beside the bed.

Ariel's parents led her away, along shadowy halls, into their own rooms. She couldn't talk. She was numb.

Her mother helped her out of her robe and into her bed by the window. Ariel took Gladly in her arms, and her mother covered them both. Then she sat beside Ariel and took her hand.

Dark, deep night lay outside the window. The bells were silent. Although she listened, Ariel heard no singing. The tree was still. She knew it would not sing again that night.

13

On the day of Aidan's funeral rain fell gently. Ariel sat between her parents in the Galilee Chapel. Fresh flowers had been arranged in the pottery jar near St. Bede's tomb, and Ariel watched a bee circling round them. Only a few people were gathered there. Mr. Langley looked very pale and sad.

"Ariel," Brother Michael had asked her the day after Aidan's death, "Aidan told me about the time you sang for him in the Galilee Chapel. Would you sing for all of us when we gather together there to remember him?"

At first Ariel thought she would not be able to do it. But the more she thought about it, the more right it seemed to be.

"Yes," she had told the monk finally. "I think I should sing for Aidan."

"Good. Do you know the setting of the Twenty-third Psalm called 'Brother James's Air'?"

"Oh yes. We sing it at home. I love it."

"That would be appropriate, don't you think so? One of our brothers plays the flute and he could accompany you."

She had practiced with the flutist, and she liked the way the flute and her own voice intertwined and filled the chapel with sound.

Now she sat waiting. On a trestle near the altar was

a plain wooden coffin. Ariel tried not to look at it. Instead she looked at the flowers in the great stone jar.

When Brother Michael nodded to her, Ariel went to stand between him and the flutist. At first she was nervous. Then she put her hand into the monk's. His hand was warm and strong, and she felt secure standing beside him. She looked at her parents and Mr. Langley. Then she began to sing:

"The Lord's my shepherd,
I'll not want . . ."

When the song had ended Brother Michael waited until the last floating sound of the flute and Ariel's voice had died away. Then he pressed her hand and nodded to her. She went to sit beside her parents again. She leaned against her father. Her mother took her hand. Ariel saw tears in her mother's eyes, but she didn't feel like crying herself. She had not yet been able to cry for Aidan.

When the service was over Mr. Langley came to speak to Ariel. "Thank you for your beautiful song. Aidan told me how much he liked hearing you sing. I'm glad you sang for him and for the rest of us once more."

"Tom," Ariel's father asked Mr. Langley, "won't you reconsider and come with us to Chartres?"

"I can't, Hugh. I belong here. I've discussed it with all the others. I must stay and make arrangements for Aidan's burial on Lindisfarne."

"I understand. This may be good-bye, then. We face a certain urgency, you know. I doubt that we'll meet again. Our work here is finished. Now we must move on."

"I know." Thomas Langley touched Ariel's head as he asked her father, "Do you leave today?"

"Yes. Right after lunch. We're driving to London this afternoon. We'll fly to Paris from there."

Ariel felt a lurch of dread. She didn't want to leave Durham. She didn't want to leave Brother Michael.

She didn't want to go to a strange city in a new country where even the language would be different.

All the rest of the morning while she was packing her things, checking to be sure she hadn't left anything, Ariel was on the verge of tears.

First I had to leave home and Robin, she thought. *Then it was Julian. Now I have to leave the cathedral and the places where I was happy with Aidan. And Brother Michael. I'll never see him again.*

After lunch while Ariel's parents loaded the car, she went to the cathedral one last time. In the Treasury Room she touched the sanctuary knocker. Then she looked at St. Cuthbert's cross, remembering the way it had looked lying on Aidan's hand, the way it had felt when she held it. Next she went into the cathedral, straight to St. Cuthbert's tomb and looked down at the polished slab. *Please, God,* she said silently, *take care of Aidan, even though You didn't heal him.* And then, thinking of her friend, she began to cry.

She was glad she was alone. But soon she realized that she was not alone, after all. Brother Michael stood beside her. He held her hand while she sobbed. Finally he wiped her face with a white handkerchief which he took from a pocket deep inside his robe. "Shall we sit together quietly for a while?" he asked her.

They sat beside each other and gradually Ariel stopped crying, but her sorrow still lay heavily upon her.

"I have a small gift for you." The monk handed her a box.

She opened it. Inside was a small bronze replica of the sanctuary knocker. She touched it. "Thank you," she said. "I can carry it all the time and touch it whenever I need to, can't I?" Without waiting for an answer she asked, "Do you think it's a devil or a lion? I can't decide."

"I personally think it is a lion," Brother Michael

said, "because the lion is a symbol of great strength and courage. Your own name means 'The Lion of God,' does it not?"

"Yes, but I don't feel brave or strong. I just feel sad. Aidan's dead and now we have to leave you and the cathedral. I don't want to go. I'm afraid I'll never see you again." She touched the bronze lion and struggled against tears.

"That may be. But although miles may part us, we will always be friends. I will speak of you and think of you each day, and you must do the same of me. Then we will be bound together always, even though we may seem to be parted."

"Why did Aidan have to die?" Ariel asked. "He didn't want to."

The monk was silent for a long moment. Then he asked, "Do you think Aidan was afraid at the last?"

"No. He wasn't afraid anymore after that day here at St. Cuthbert's tomb. And he smiled before he died. Do you think he saw something?"

"What do you think about that?"

"He wanted to tell me something. But he didn't have time. I think he smiled because he saw something beautiful. But I don't know what it was." Ariel found that talking about Aidan with the monk made it easier to bear his death.

"I, too, think he saw something beautiful," Brother Michael said. "We can't know what it was, of course, but we can be glad for him. We grieve because he is no longer here with us, and it is right to grieve." He touched Ariel's hand. "Try to remember that."

"I will." Ariel knew that the time had come for her to leave, but she had to ask one more question. "Brother Michael, have you ever heard a tree sing?"

A smile touched his eyes as he answered her. "Yes, I have heard a tree singing. Now we share a secret, you and Aidan and I."

She sighed. He understood everything. Together they left the cathedral and went to the castle. The Marsdens were standing by the car.

"We were going to come looking for you," Ariel's mother said. "We're ready to leave now. Are you?"

"Yes." Ariel looked at Brother Michael. "Good-bye. I'll never forget you."

"Nor will I forget you."

Ariel watched from the back window of the car. Brother Michael stood, his hand lifted, as they drove away. She watched the cathedral towers grow smaller. She watched until she could no longer see them, standing firm and strong against the sky. Until she could no longer hear the bells.

Good-bye, Durham, she thought. *Good-bye, Brother Michael. Good-bye, Aidan.* She held Gladly against her face and felt the smooth softness of his fur. And she touched the sanctuary knocker.

14

Later, Ariel could remember hardly anything about the drive from Durham to London. She was so tired that she slept most of the way. She could hardly rouse herself enough to step into reality when her mother said, "Ariel, we're in London. Can you wake up now and help carry your luggage into the hotel?"

She struggled to keep her eyes open. She picked up her flight bag and Gladly and followed her parents into the lobby of the hotel. "Will Mr. Herauld be here?" she asked.

"We don't expect to see him here," her father said. "Are you awake now?"

She tried to smile at him, but her face muscles didn't want to work, so she only nodded. "I guess so."

"You'll feel better after you stretch and walk a bit, and after some supper." Her father registered at the desk and the three of them took a small elevator up to their room. A lift, the desk clerk called it.

A large and a small bedroom were separated by a bathroom. Ariel had the smaller room. She looked at the bed and longed to fall into it. *Maybe,* she thought, *if I could go to sleep again, we'd be back in Durham when I wake up, with everything the way it was. Or maybe we'd be home again.* But she really knew that none of that would happen.

She felt that she was sleepwalking while she and her parents strolled on the busy streets of London. She thought the people who hurried along those streets looked tired, even angry. She glanced at the newspaper headlines. Over and over again she saw the words ARMS RACE and WORLD TENSION INCREASES. She pushed the thought of those words far back into the corner of her mind. She would not think about them.

She could barely hold her fork when they ate supper in the hotel restaurant. She heard her mother say, "Hugh, she's practically asleep. Let's get her to bed."

Back in her room, she struggled out of her clothes and into her nightgown. When she was finally in bed she thought she heard someone say, *Better tomorrow,* just before she sank into a sleep so deep that she did not even dream.

When she awoke, sunlight was pouring through her window and she did not know where she was. She lay trying to remember. She heard the murmur of voices and then she remembered that she was in a London hotel and her parents were in the next room.

She took Gladly and went to her parents' room. They were dressed, their suitcases already packed. "Well, here she is," her father said, "awake at last."

"Feeling better?" her mother asked.

"I don't know." She only knew that she felt heavy, stupid. Not like her usual self at all, even after such a long sleep. "Maybe I'm sick."

Her mother reached to feel her forehead. "No fever," she said. "Do you really feel sick?"

"I don't know. I feel funny. Sort of . . . well, heavy. It's hard to explain."

"Maybe you're hungry. We've ordered breakfast for you. There's juice. And rolls and jam. Sound good?"

"I guess so." She didn't feel hungry. She didn't feel anything. Except tired. But when she began to eat she discovered that she was hungry, after all.

Her father was reading a newspaper. The headlines

stared at her, the letters thick and black. NUCLEAR WAR THREAT LOOMS. WILL SUMMIT BE IN TIME? She looked away from those words. Then she thought, *Aidan would tell me not to be an ostrich. But Aidan's dead, so maybe nobody will care if I don't look.*

Still, she asked her father, "Is there going to be a war?"

Her father looked grave. "No one can tell, Ariel. Things look bad just now. It's a complicated situation. It's hard to say which way things are going to go."

"I want to go home." Ariel felt that she could not stand any more traveling, any more time away from her own house, from Robin. And she thought she could not stand any more pain—the kind of pain she felt at Aidan's death.

Her mother said, "Darling, we know it's been a terribly hard time for you. You've been incredibly brave. We all have to go on being brave, even when things are as frightening as these headlines. We're leaving here as soon as you are ready. We're going to fly to Paris and then take a train to Chartres."

Her father said, "We had hoped to spend some time showing you Paris, but now we find that we must go right on to Chartres. It will be a long, hard day. We'll both help you as much as we can."

Her father was right. It was a hard day. More than once Ariel touched the sanctuary knocker. The short flight to Paris was on a crowded plane, and Ariel sat beside her mother while her father sat far behind them.

From the airport they took a cab to the railway station, which was even more confusing because all the signs were in French and the sharp voices spoke in French.

Everyone seemed to be in a hurry. Faces looked strained and anxious. On the train from Paris to Chartres she sat ahead of her parents beside a woman who was reading. She did not once look at Ariel or speak to her.

Ariel was feeling hot, tired, and cross when, almost at the end of the short trip, she saw them. The spires of the cathedral. They were not like the towers of Durham, sturdy and firm. These two spires were slender and pointed. They seemed to stab the sky. She was surprised to see that the two spires did not match each other.

Suddenly she wasn't tired anymore. She was only excited. She knelt up on the seat and faced her parents. "Do you see them? The spires? They're just like the pictures."

The woman beside her put down her book and said to Ariel, *"C'est la cathédrale. C'est plus belle, n'est-ce-pas?"*

Ariel's father said to her, "She's asking you if you don't think the cathedral is very beautiful."

Ariel turned to the French woman. "Oh yes. I can hardly wait to go there."

The woman nodded and smiled, as if she understood what Ariel was saying.

"We're coming in to Chartres now," her mother said. "Do you have everything?"

She followed her parents off the train and through the station. They walked to the hotel which was directly across from the Post Office. It was not a long walk, but it was uphill and the sun was hot. Ariel was glad to step inside the small lobby where it was much cooler. Her father spoke easily in French to the attractive young woman at the desk.

When he had registered, the woman spoke to Ariel in English which was accented in a charming way. "Here is a letter which has been waiting for you." She handed Ariel an envelope.

Ariel looked at the return address. "It's from Robin," she told her parents. "She remembered to write to me."

"Of course," her mother said. "She promised, didn't she?"

"Yes." Then Ariel rather shyly spoke to the woman at the desk. *"Merci beaucoup,"* she said. "Thank you very much. It's from my best friend."

"Ah, bien." The woman smiled. "Very good. It is nice to hear from one's friends when one is parted from them."

The Marsdens walked up a short flight of stairs to their rooms. Again Ariel had a small room separated from her parents' larger room by a bath. She sat on the bed and opened Robin's letter.

"Dear Ariel,

"I miss you. It seems as if you've been gone forever. I've been sitting with the sugar babies a lot and it helps to have the money. But those kids! You wouldn't believe what they did last time, so I won't even tell you.

"Your postcard came from that island. It looks pretty old and rundown to me, but you seemed to like it, so it must be OK. I wish you were here. Nothing much is happening.

"Ned is all excited because he thinks we're going to have a war with Russia. I hope not. Remember all those horrible things Mr. Long told us about nuclear bombs? Why would anybody be dumb enough to want to start a war like that?

"Write to me again. Hug Gladly for me and tell your folks Hi. I'll be thinking about you on your birthday.

"Love, Robin."

There it was again, the talk about war. Ariel did not want to think about it. She didn't want to think about her birthday either, only a few days away.

She looked out her bedroom window into a courtyard below. Two children were swinging, calling happily to each other in a language Ariel did not understand. She could not see the cathedral spires.

"Shall I unpack everything?" she called to her mother.

"Unpack just what you need for tonight and tomorrow," her mother said, stepping into Ariel's room. "We're not going to be here long. Our house will be ready for us soon."

"A house? Why do we need a house? How long are we going to stay?"

"We still aren't sure," her mother said.

"Come on, women." Her father poked his head into the room. "Doesn't anyone want to see the cathedral?"

"I'm ready," Ariel said. "Can we go now?"

"*Allons, alors,*" her father said cheerfully. "Let's go."

15

Ariel and her parents walked toward the cathedral, guided by the spires which pointed to the sky. They walked past the Post Office, past small shops, past a cafe where people were eating at tables on the sidewalk, under brightly colored umbrellas. They walked along a street lined with trees, covered with gravel, always moving toward the spires.

And then there it was at the end of a long cement walkway where it had stood for centuries. The cathedral, slender and delicate, its two spires rising so high that Ariel had to lean far back to see the tops of them.

She had been right. The towers didn't match. The one on the left was lacy, decorated with small pointed arches and ornaments which Ariel couldn't quite make out. The other one was plain, rising like a giant cone to its pointed top, crowned with a cross.

"It's like a palace," Ariel said. "It's like a palace for a princess." She stared at the building which lifted toward Heaven. Durham Cathedral was solid and sturdy, sitting firmly on the ground. It was like a grand, mighty fortress and Ariel loved it.

But this cathedral was different. It seemed almost to float. Or it seemed to sail, like a great stone ship outlined against the sky, the two spires its masts.

As she looked, Ariel began to notice statues on the slender columns of the building: statues of men and women whose faces were calm and kind. They looked alive, as if they might speak at any moment. Only their eyes were vacant—stone eyes which looked past Ariel at something she couldn't see. It did not matter that they were weather-worn or damaged. She knew they were real people.

"Who are they, Daddy?" she whispered. The whole building made her want to whisper.

"They represent the kings and queens of Judah," her father said, "the ancestors of Christ."

Ariel knew at once which statue she would return to again and again. Ariel would have known that person was royal even if her father had not told her, for she wore a crown. Her hair was parted in the center and lay in two smooth braids which reached below her knees. Her gown was soft with tiny pleats. It fell to her feet and it had long, gracefully flowing sleeves. Ariel could hardly believe she was looking at stone, not cloth. The lady held a book in one hand. The other hand was missing, but Ariel was sure it had pointed up.

Her face was beautiful, even though the nose was broken. She smiled faintly, as if she had a secret. Ariel had a feeling that the lady resembled someone she knew. Then it came to her.

"She looks like you, Mother. If you had long hair like that, you'd look like her. She's so beautiful."

Ariel's mother hugged her. "I think that's the nicest thing anyone ever said to me."

"What's her name?" Ariel asked her father.

"No one knows."

Then I'll call you Emilie, Ariel thought. *Princess Emilie. Even though you are a queen, I'll call you a princess, because you look like one to me.*

While they stood together looking at the stone woman, a young boy ran toward them, past them. When he came to the statues he jumped high into the air, trying to touch the feet of Ariel's lady. Again and again he jumped calling, "Lady. Lady."

"Come, Isaac," a man said to him. "Come. She's too high. Remember? You can't reach her."

But the little boy only laughed and continued to jump, trying to touch the statue, calling over and over, "Lady. Lady."

Ariel thought, *I know how he feels. I'd like to touch her, too.* She thought the boy seemed different somehow. His face was merry, but his eyes were ... different. His body was loose as he bounced and jumped.

The man who had called to him went and picked him up, holding him as if he were a baby, whirling him around and around, making him laugh. Soon the child said, "Down, Papa. Down."

His father put him down and steadied him. The boy stared at Ariel. She looked at him and smiled. "Hi," she said. But he only stared. She thought he looked about the age of the sugar babies. They were five. This boy could be older or younger. It was hard to tell. But Ariel knew she liked him.

The father took his son's hand and said to Ariel, "You were studying my son's favorite statue, I believe."

"Yes, sir. I think she's beautiful."

"So does Isaac. He greets her each time we come here. I think he expects her to speak to him one day." Then he turned to Ariel's parents. "I am Aaron Steiner. You have already observed my son, Isaac."

Ariel thought Mr. Steiner looked like a man in a book. He was short and stocky. His hair and beard were black and curly, his eyes dark and kind. Something about him reminded Ariel of Brother Michael, but it had nothing to do with appearance or speech. She only knew there was something.

Ariel's father shook Mr. Steiner's hand. "Our name is Marsden. Hugh, Emilie, and Ariel."

Then, suddenly, Isaac took Ariel's hand and began to

pull her toward the central door of the cathedral. "Now," he said. "Now. Lights."

Ariel asked Isaac's father, "What does he mean? What does he want?"

"Shall we go inside?" Mr. Steiner asked. "Then you'll see what he means. Have you been inside yet?"

"Not yet," Ariel told him. "We just got here."

"From Durham," Hugh Marsden said.

"Ah yes. Durham." Mr. Steiner looked thoughtful. "Is Brother Michael well?"

"Brother Michael?" Ariel was surprised and happy. "You know him?"

"Yes. We have known each other for many years." A look passed between Mr. Steiner and Ariel's father. It was the kind of look which meant a secret. "Shall we go inside now?" Mr. Steiner took his son's hand.

Somehow Ariel felt that stepping inside the cathedral would be like stepping into a new world. And it was. Even Isaac was quiet for a moment. Ariel took a long, deep breath and looked around her. In the dim light her eyes were drawn to stone pillars which looked slender and fragile. Yet they appeared to be holding up the entire building.

She looked up, following the lines of the pillars. She could barely see the top, the roof was so far away. Higher and higher the slim pillars reached, curving at last to help form the roof.

And then Ariel saw that the walls were filled with windows of colored glass. They gleamed with red, green, gold, and blues so vivid that they danced before her eyes. She was only faintly aware that the windows contained pictures formed by the many-colored pieces of glass.

Isaac pulled at Ariel's hand and said, "Lights. Lights."

Late-afternoon sun touched the glass, breaking colors into prisms, making rainbows of light on walls, columns, and floor. She knew what Isaac meant.

It's magic, she thought. *It really is. I wish Aidan were here. I wish he could see it. It's like fairyland. Or maybe it's like Heaven.*

Isaac ran about trying to catch bits of the rainbow-light. He laughed and jumped with pure joy when his hands were stained with color.

Mr. Steiner said, "I hope he does not disturb too much in this sacred place. Do you think so?" He turned toward Ariel's mother. "We would never wish to be a disturbance. He is, as you see, a happy boy."

Emilie Marsden said, "I can't see him disturbing anyone. He is a most appealing child. How old is he? About six?"

"Yes. He has passed his sixth birthday. In some ways he will never be any older than he is now. But I hope he will always be happy."

"His name is appropriate," Ariel's father said.

"What does it mean?" Ariel asked Mr. Steiner.

"Isaac translates into 'Laughter.' " A shadow crossed Mr. Steiner's face as he said, "My wife was well past forty when she conceived. We decided that we would call the child Sarah if she were a girl and Isaac if we had a son. When he was born, Isaac was our laughter and our joy. Like the joy of Abraham and Sarah. But my wife did not live to see our son grow. She died during the second month of his life."

Like Aidan, Ariel thought. *His mother died, too.* Sadness washed over her as the memory of Aidan filled her thoughts, and she looked at Isaac's laughing face through her own sudden tears.

"The cathedral is locked at seven," Mr. Steiner told them, "and it is not open at night unless there is a service or a concert. But one needs to see it at all hours of the day and night. It is constantly changing, full of miracles."

"Shall we leave now?" Ariel's father asked her. "We can come back early in the morning and stay as long as we like."

"Yes. Let's go." Suddenly Ariel was very tired.

Her fatigue must have showed because her mother said, "It's been quite a day. Let's go back to the hotel and have an early dinner. We'll get to bed early. We all need a rest."

Mr. Steiner and Isaac walked away from the cathedral with them. Soon Isaac put his hand in Ariel's and trotted along beside her, leaving her now and again to pick up a pebble or a twig. Once he ran up to Ariel holding a bird's feather, black and shiny. He offered it to her. "Here, Girl," he said.

She took it from him. "Thank you, Isaac. My name is Ariel. Can you say Ariel?"

He ran away from her laughing. "Girl, Girl, Girl," he chanted.

Mr. Steiner said, "Ariel, one day he may surprise you by saying your name. But then again, he may not. With Isaac one can never be sure."

"That's all right, Mr. Steiner," Ariel assured him. "He can call me Girl. I don't mind."

As if he knew they had been talking about him, Isaac ran toward them again. He planted himself in front of Ariel so that she could not move. Then he said, "Girl, kiss good-bye."

She knelt to his level. He kissed her cheek. She hugged him and said, "Good-bye, Isaac. Maybe I'll see you tomorrow."

"You've made a friend," Mr. Steiner told her. "Isaac will be totally loyal to you now. That's his way."

I'll be loyal to him, too, she thought. *Maybe he can be a sort of little brother. Maybe I can help take care of him.*

16

"Light, Papa. Light." Isaac buried his head on his father's shoulder and whimpered. Ariel thought she knew how he felt. The crypt was dark and menacing, far beneath the cathedral and she, too, thought she'd like to escape up into the light.

"It will be all right, Isaac." His father soothed him. "Father André is going to show us something beautiful." But Isaac would not look up.

"Does Father André know where he's going?" Ariel whispered to her mother.

"Oh yes. He knows every inch of this cathedral. He won't let us get lost."

"Look, Isaac." Father André pointed to a small altar which stood on a low platform under a stone arch. A colorful hanging was suspended from the top of the arch, falling to the altar itself. Displayed against the hanging was the figure of a seated woman holding a child.

"Lady," Isaac said, looking up from the shelter of his father's arms. "Lady."

"He always responds to representations of Mary," Father André said. "And you never try to dissuade him."

"Of course not." Mr. Steiner smiled. "She was a good Jewess, was she not? And a good mother, too."

The priest had unlocked the gate which led to the crypt and had guided his little group down along dark passages, into this small chapel. At first Ariel was afraid. Now she was beginning to feel better.

"This is the largest crypt in France," their guide told them. "Come along."

They followed him along the dark passages. Ariel stayed close beside her parents.

"How would you like to sleep down here?" Father André asked Ariel.

She shuddered. "I wouldn't. It's too cold and dark."

"People did sleep here," he told them. "This is where the pilgrims slept when they came to the cathedral. Sometimes they were sick and they stayed down here a good while, being cared for, until they were able to go on."

"I wouldn't have liked it," Ariel said.

"Even though it does seem gloomy," Father Andre said, "I can picture it with hundreds of candles burning. With the singing of the pilgrims, with their great joy at having arrived at the place of their heart's desire." Then he smiled at Ariel. "I wouldn't like to stay here, either, as a matter of fact. But it seems they did."

"Could you get lost down here?" Ariel asked.

"Yes, unless you knew the building very well. You see, it follows the shape of the cathedral. There's plenty of opportunity for taking wrong turns. Never try to come down here alone. Not that anyone would allow you to. One must have a key."

"I wouldn't want to." Ariel shivered again.

"Will you please stay right here with Isaac for just a little while?" Mr. Steiner asked Ariel. "We need to consult with Father André about a few things. We won't be far away."

Ariel and Isaac stood together near a spot of light thrown by a single electric bulb which was fastened to the wall. Isaac was unusually quiet, content to hold Ariel's hand and wait.

Ariel could hear the murmur of the adults' voices, but she could not hear what they were saying. *It's that secret again,* she thought. *I wish they'd tell me what's happening. They hurried me away from home to get to Durham. Then we had to leave Durham in a hurry, and nothing's happened yet to explain it. When will they tell me?*

Isaac began to whimper again. "It's all right," Ariel told him. "Don't be afraid." But he put his arms around her waist and clung to her. "Listen, Isaac," she said, "do you like this song?"

She sang the old French dancing song which she had heard that day in her father's class at home. Almost at once Isaac relaxed and looked up at her with his special smile. He began to dance around her with his loose, clumsy steps.

The others joined them while Ariel was still singing. "Where did you learn that tune?" the priest asked her.

"In one of my father's classes. I wish I knew the words. I can only sing the melody."

Her father and the priest smiled at each other. "It's just as well that you don't know the words," Father André said. "Enjoy that lilting tune and wait till you're older to learn the words. There's time enough. Right, Mr. Marsden?"

"*Vraiment,*" Ariel's father said. "Twelve is too young to be in love."

"I'm nearly thirteen," Ariel protested.

"Sing, Girl!" Isaac ordered.

"Ariel will sing for you again later, I'm sure," his father told him. "We're going up now."

It was good to be out in the fresh air again after the musty darkness of the crypt. Tourists swarmed about, some with guidebooks, some with binoculars, some with ice-cream cones.

"Sometimes they try to bring their food into the cathedral," Father André grumbled. "They forget it's a church, not a café." Then he asked, "Would you like to look at the windows again?"

"I know Isaac would," Mr. Steiner said.

They followed Father André inside. At first all Ariel could see was a mixture of brilliant colors. Blue, emerald-green, scarlet, and gold shone from the wall, their hues so bright that Ariel almost felt she could hear them.

Isaac ran about trying to catch prisms. No one tried to stop him.

As they stood there, a young girl came up to Father André and spoke to him rapidly in French. Ariel could not understand what she said.

"*Merci*, Anne-Marie. Please tell your mother I'll be right there." The girl hurried off as the priest said, "I'm sorry. I have to leave you now. Anne-Marie's mother works in the bookshop and she says I have an urgent message." Before he strode away from them he said to Ariel, "Anne-Marie will be a good friend to you. She and her mother live in the house directly across from the one where you'll be living." Then he was gone.

"How does he know where we're going to live?" she asked her father.

"He found the house for us. And speaking of that, we need to settle in. I'll meet you there with the luggage, Emilie," he said. They had packed at the hotel that morning after breakfast. "I'll take a cab and be along presently."

Ariel and her mother went together to their new home. They walked along behind the cathedral, past many small shops. In the window of one Ariel saw cheese and pickles, in another, fruit. A third shop sold meat and still another sold bread and pastries. Everything looked good.

At last they came to a street which led down a rather steep hill. They walked down the hill on the cobblestone street and stopped in front of a house which surprised Ariel. She had never seen one like it.

The street was extremely narrow and the house was too. It rose high and slender above the street, decorated with slender strips of timber and with narrow windows here and there. Marigolds blossomed in pots on the wide sills. Ariel saw that there was not a single tree.

I want my own house, Ariel thought, *and my oak tree. I want to be home.* Aloud she asked, "How long do we have to stay here? Don't you know, really?"

"I honestly don't," her mother said. "But don't you think it's a nice little house? Living in a French house is going to be an adventure."

"I suppose so," Ariel said reluctantly. "Have you been inside?"

"No. We'll all go in together. It's a very old house which has been restored so that it will be comfortable," her mother explained. "It was built in the fifteenth century. Those narrow slats on the walls are called half-timbers."

While they stood looking and talking, a cab drew up before the house. Ariel's father and the cab driver took out the luggage, the driver cheerful and friendly, although Ariel couldn't understand what he said because he spoke so rapidly.

"Will I ever be able to understand French people?" she whispered to her mother. "They talk so fast."

"I know," her mother said. "I have trouble, too."

Hugh Marsden unlocked the door. *"Entrez, Madame et Mademoiselle,"* he said with a low bow. "Enter."

They entered through a small foyer into a spacious living room. "It's charming." Emilie Marsden looked around the room. It was decorated in blue with touches of rose and cream. Someone had arranged roses in a pewter bowl and placed them on a polished table.

"I want to see my room," Ariel said.

"The bedrooms must be upstairs." Her father led the way.

"This one is ours, I guess." Her mother stepped into a large room. A four-poster bed was draped with a blue canopy, and the furniture smelled of lemon-scented polish.

Ariel went across the hall to see the room which was to be hers. From the window she could look down on the cobbled street. She could also see a room in the house across the street. The curtains were pulled back, the shutters open.

A girl stood at the window looking out at her, the girl who had brought Father André his message in the cathedral. For a moment they stared at each other. Then the girl waved to Ariel. Ariel waved, too. The French girl pointed down toward the street. Ariel nodded and ran down the stairs and into the narrow street. The girl was waiting for her.

"Hi," Ariel said.

"How do you do?" the girl asked formally.

"I'm Ariel Marsden."

"My name is Anne-Marie Leclerc. You are from America, are you not?"

"Yes. We live in California."

"It must be very lovely there."

Ariel thought for a moment. "It's a lot like it is here except that we have palm trees and you don't have any smog. At least, I haven't seen any."

"Smog? What is this smog?"

Ariel wrinkled her nose. "It's when the air is so full of chemicals and stuff that you can't breathe and your eyes sting."

"That must be most unpleasant." Anne-Marie studied Ariel and then asked, "How many years have you?"

Ariel frowned in concentration.

Anne-Marie tried again. "How old have you?"

"Oh. I'll be thirteen the day after tomorrow."

Anne-Marie smiled. "I am already thirteen. Last month I had a birthday."

Ariel sighed. "I was going to have a party, but we came here instead. My best friend and I had it all planned."

"I am sorry," Anne-Marie said. "You must be disappointed. And you must miss your friend."

"Yes. I miss her," Ariel said. Then she added, "You speak very good English. I wish I could speak French. I only know a few words."

"You will learn. I will help you with French and you must help me with English. I am taught English in school, but I do not often have a chance to speak with an American. Now, please, will you come in and meet my mother? She is at home for lunch. We were told that you were to live on our street. *Maman* will be happy to meet you."

Anne-Marie led Ariel through the front of the house to a cheery kitchen. Copper pots and pans hung against the wall, and flowering plants and herbs grew in pots on the windowsills.

"*Maman,* this is Ariel Marsden from America. From California." Anne-Marie pronounced Ariel's name with the accent on the last syllable . . . Ariél . . . and it sounded very French.

Madame Leclerc shook hands formally with Ariel. "We are so glad you have come to Chartres. Anne-Marie has never had a young friend so near."

She was a small woman, not much taller than her daughter. But while Anne-Marie's complexion was fair and her eyes blue, Madame Leclerc's skin was golden-tan and her eyes were so dark they looked black. Anne-Marie's fair hair was drawn back into one thick braid. Her mother's straight black hair was cut in bangs above those dark eyes. She wore a simple rose-colored dress. Ariel thought she was beautiful.

"And now," Anne-Marie's mother said, "will you

please go and ask your parents if you will all join us for lunch? It is difficult, the first day in a strange house, to arrange for meals. We will be pleased to have you lunch with us." Madame Leclerc's pronunciation was perfect. Only the accent which Ariel liked so much suggested that English was not her own language.

Ariel ran across the narrow street and burst into the living room where her parents sat quietly together. They looked at each other with that stunned expression which she had seen before. She knew they were terribly worried about something. And they still had not told her what it was.

She broke in on their silence. "We're invited to lunch. It's Anne-Marie, the girl at the cathedral. Her mother works there. They want us all to come to lunch. Now. Please. They're so nice." She was out of breath.

"What a kind thing for them to suggest." Emilie Marsden stood, holding out her hands to her husband. "Come along, Hugh." He took her hands and she playfully pulled him up. "*Allons*. Come, let's go meet our new neighbors."

Even though her mother pretended to be happy, Ariel was sure that the terrible *something* still hung over all of them.

17

On her thirteenth birthday Ariel woke to the sound
of bells. For just a moment she thought she was in
Durham. *Maybe Aidan and I can take a boat ride on the
river,* she thought.

Then she remembered.

Aidan was dead. She was in Chartres. It was her
birthday. Robin was half a world away. No friends, no
party. Not even her own familiar room. And something
dreadful hanging over her and her parents.

She looked around her. A shaft of sunlight touched
one side of the wallpaper, turning the gray stripes silver, making the small garlands of flowers glow.

Happy Birthday to me, anyway, she thought. She
hugged Gladly and said, "We'll just have to pretend to
be happy. They're worried enough without any more
complaining from me."

She dressed and went downstairs. Her father sat
reading a newspaper. Ariel was glad she couldn't read
French. She didn't want to see the headlines today.

Hugh Marsden looked up and smiled at his daughter.
"Happy Birthday," he said. "Come kiss an old man who
suddenly has a teenage child."

She sat on the arm of his chair and leaned to kiss
him. "You're not old, Daddy. Where's Mother?"

"Gone to get fresh rolls. She thought she'd be back
before you got up."

As he spoke, Emilie Marsden stepped into the room,

bringing the aroma of fresh bread with her. "Happy Birthday, darling." She kissed Ariel. "I wish you could have smelled the bakery this morning. It was heavenly. There's absolutely nothing like the smell of freshly baked bread. If they made a perfume like that, I'd wear it."

They sat down to breakfast together. The table was set with blue place mats and napkins which were embroidered with small flowers. The design reminded Ariel of her bedroom wallpaper. The fresh, warm rolls were delicious, spread with peach jam. Ariel had a cup of very weak *café-au-lait*.

"I'll give you more *lait* than *café*." Her mother poured hot milk and coffee from two white pitchers. Ariel liked the way the liquids looked as they merged to fill her cup.

After the meal they went to the living room to begin their traditional birthday ceremony. Ariel chose a chair and sat in it like a princess on her throne, her loyal subjects around her.

"Mail or presents first?" her father asked.

"Mail, I guess." Ariel liked to save her presents for last, prolonging the anticipation. And she wanted this birthday morning to be as much like home as possible. Then perhaps she could forget for a while the thing which threatened them all.

Her father handed her an envelope.

"It's from Robin." She read the note aloud.

"I got your letter. I'm sorry that boy died. He sounded nice."

Ariel looked at her mother. Her eyes met Ariel's in sympathy and understanding.

Ariel continued to read. "I saw Kevin yesterday. He looks the same except that now the streak down the middle is bright purple instead of green. He's a mess. Write to me again. I miss you. Love, Robin."

I miss you, too, Ariel thought.

The next note was from Aidan's father. "Happy Birthday, Ariel. Sing and be happy. Thomas Langley."

Ariel swallowed the lump that rose in her throat.

Finally she opened a note from Brother Michael. He wrote, "On this anniversary of your birth I wish you peace, joy, and your heart's desire. And I congratulate your parents upon their excellent choice of a daughter. Always your friend, Brother Michael."

"I miss him," Ariel said. "I wish he were here right now."

"That would be nice," her mother agreed.

"I thought maybe Julian would write to me," Ariel said. "I gave her the address of the hotel. Maybe the letter is there. Could we ask later?"

"If you like," her mother said. "Now, which package first?"

Ariel pointed to a large flat package wrapped in white and tied with yellow yarn. "That one. I can't guess what's in it."

Her mother handed it to her. "It's from me with a great deal of love."

Ariel opened the package carefully. For a long time she stared at the gift. She couldn't find the words she wanted to say. Finally she looked up. "Oh, Mother," she said. "Oh, Mother!"

Aidan's face looked out at her. He stood beside the Celtic cross on Lindisfarne, the branches of the tree bending around him. His eyes looked into her own. She thought she might hear him speak if she were quiet long enough, the pen-and-ink drawing was so lifelike.

"When did you do it?" she asked her mother.

"I began the sketch that day on Lindisfarne. Remember?"

"Yes. In the tea shop."

"That's right. Mostly I drew Aidan from memory. I'm glad you like it. I wasn't sure whether it would make you sad or happy to have it."

"Both," Ariel told her. "But mostly it makes me happy. This is the way I remember him." She left her temporary throne to embrace her mother. "Thank you," she whispered. "It's wonderful."

"Next?" her father asked as she returned to her place of honor.

"That little one. The smallest box."

Her father handed her the package. Inside was a pendant on a thin silver chain. It was an enameled rose, small and perfect with delicate green leaves and stem.

She gasped. "Daddy, it's beautiful."

"I'm glad you like it. I chose it when we were in London. I thought it was time for you to have an adult ornament, now that you are in your teens."

"I love it. I love both my presents. Thank you."

Her mother left the room saying, "I'll be right back. Don't go away." Then, from the top of the stairs she called, "Close your eyes."

Obediently, Ariel shut her eyes.

In a moment her mother said, "All right. You can open them now."

Ariel's mother stood before her holding up a white dress. It was full-length with narrow straps. The broad hem was embroidered with a pattern of intertwining flowers and leaves. It was the dress she had described to her mother, the one she had wanted for her party.

"It's the most perfect dress I've ever seen," she said, wondering where she'd wear it. "It's exactly what I wanted. And the necklace will be perfect with it." She ran to hug her parents. "Thank you," she said. "Thank you for a wonderful birthday."

"You can wear it tonight," her mother told her. "A few people are coming in. Madame Leclerc and Anne-Marie. Mr. Steiner and Isaac. And some others."

Ariel was pleased. "Then I'll have a party after all." But when she saw the look that passed between her parents, she knew that this would not be the usual kind of birthday party. Not the kind she had planned.

"There's something else," her father said. "All along we've promised to tell you what you've wanted to know about this trip. Tonight you will learn all that we know, and perhaps more."

"Really?" Ariel looked at her father in surprise. "Tonight?"

"Yes. Tonight."

For a fleeting moment Ariel wondered if she wanted to know, after all. It must be something terrible to make everyone so unhappy. But she knew she had to learn about it, whatever it was.

After trying on her new dress, which fit perfectly, Ariel asked her mother, "May I go to the cathedral to meet Anne-Marie? She has some things to show me."

"Fine. Have a good time, and please be back in time for lunch."

"OK." Ariel followed the spires to the cathedral. Anne-Marie was waiting for her in the bookshop, as she had promised.

Madame Leclerc saw Ariel first. *"Bonjour, Ariel."*

"Bonjour, Madame," Ariel said rather shyly.

"Ariel," Anne-Marie said, *"Bon Anniversaire.* That means Happy Birthday. Now we are the same age, are we not?"

"You are going to explore the cathedral together now?" Anne-Marie's mother asked.

"Yes, *Maman.* I wish to show Ariel some of our treasures."

"Have a happy morning." Madame Leclerc turned to wait on a customer who had selected postcards.

"I'll get some cards to send to Robin," Ariel told Anne-Marie. "Later, I guess."

"Robin is your friend at home?" Anne-Marie asked.

"Yes. My best friend."

At first the two girls were a bit stiff with each other,

although Ariel liked the French girl. Still, she was very different from Robin. More formal, more dignified. She seemed older than thirteen.

Anne-Marie asked, "Do you not think our cathedral is beautiful?"

"Oh yes. It's wonderful. I loved it right away, as soon as I saw it from the train window. And I love it more all the time. Have you been to Durham Cathedral?"

"That is in England?" Anne-Marie asked. "I have not been to England. Someday, though, I hope to be able to travel. I would like to visit California, too."

"I hope you can," Ariel said. "You could stay with us."

"That is a kind invitation. But it will not be for a very long time. You see, my father died two years ago, and our life is not the same. We have not much money."

"I'm sorry about your father. Robin misses her father, too. He isn't dead, but her parents are divorced. So Robin doesn't see him very often."

"I am sorry."

Ariel asked her, "Do you know Isaac Steiner?"

"Oh yes, we all know Isaac. We all love him." She looked at Ariel quickly as if to challenge her.

"I do, too," Ariel said. "And I'm glad he likes me." She felt that it was important to Anne-Marie to know how she felt about Isaac. "I think it's sad that he has no mother. There are so many sad things."

"Yes. And the most sad thing I ever experienced was the death of my father. He was an architect. He said that the men who made this building so long ago knew everything about architecture. He admired them greatly." She sighed. "Sometimes I think of this cathedral as my home," Anne-Marie said. "All the sculptured figures seem to me as if they are part of my family. Does that sound foolish?"

"Oh no," Ariel said.

Anne-Marie pointed out the figures in some of the

windows. Ariel had to lean far back to see them. "The blue glass is said to be the finest in the world," the French girl said.

"I love the colors." Ariel smiled at Anne-Marie. "So does Isaac."

"Yes. I like to watch him try to catch the prisms." Anne-Marie led Ariel around the cathedral, pointing out carvings, pillars, arches. The building was so vast, so imposing that even with Anne-Marie beside her, Ariel suddenly felt lost. She felt homesickness rise in her and overflow like a flood. She swallowed hard.

Anne-Marie looked at her and said, "Something is wrong. I can see it in your face."

"It's just that I get homesick," Ariel explained. "I know it's silly, especially when my parents are right here in Chartres."

"I know just how you feel," Anne-Marie assured her. "One summer I went to be with my aunt and my cousins at their home by the sea and I thought that I should die of loneliness. Everything was so different. I missed my parents terribly. I was made to feel welcome there, you understand. But it simply was not the same."

The sympathy in the French girl's tone made Ariel feel better. "Sometimes I just can't help it. Robin and I had a really special party planned for today. Besides, something's going on this summer that I don't understand. I can't help being worried. Something's awfully wrong."

Anne-Marie studied her with clear blue eyes. "And our parents will not tell us what it is. Often I feel that it is most unfair. I am surely old enough to share with my mother whatever it is that makes her so unhappy. But she will not tell me."

A wave of relief replaced Ariel's flood of homesickness. Her new friend had the same worries. She could be trusted. Impulsively Ariel said, "I'd like to show you something. Will you come with me?"

Anne-Marie followed her outside to the Royal Portal. Ariel pointed to the crowned, long-haired lady. "I don't know her name. My father says she represents a queen. I think she looks like my mother. I call her Princess Emilie. Isn't she beautiful?"

"*Oui. Elle est très, très belle.*" Anne-Marie shot Ariel a sideways glance. "Do you understand what I said?"

"I think you said, 'Yes. She is very, very beautiful.'"

"*Très bon.* Very good. I told you that you would soon understand French. And you will soon speak it well, too, I am sure."

Before Ariel left Anne-Marie to go home for lunch she said, "I had a wonderful time. Thank you. *Merci beaucoup.* I'll see you tonight at our house."

"*Oui. Maman* and I look forward to the evening."

Then Ariel said, "I'll tell you a secret. Tonight we are going to find out what's going on. My parents promised."

Anne-Marie looked worried. "All at once I wonder whether I really want to know. What if it is something terrible?"

"I think it is," Ariel said slowly, "and I wondered the same thing. But we have to know, don't we? Whatever it is, we have to know."

18

The first to arrive that evening was Mr. Steiner carrying Isaac. Hugh Marsden greeted them at the door. "Aaron, welcome. Hello, Isaac. How are you this evening?" But the child hid his face against his father's shoulder.

Ariel came down the stairs and saw them standing there. "Hello, Mr. Steiner. Hi, Isaac. Will you come and sit by me?" She held out her hand.

Isaac did not respond. Mr. Steiner said, "How very lovely you look, Ariel. That is a most becoming dress. And what a beautiful pendant."

"Thank you. They're birthday presents."

"Is this your birthday?"

"Yes. I'm thirteen today."

"Congratulations. You look most grown-up. Perhaps Isaac does not recognize you yet."

"It's pretty different from jeans and a tee shirt," Ariel said. "Come on, Isaac. It's just me." She tried to coax the little boy, but he refused to look at her.

"It is curious," Aaron Steiner said to Ariel and her father. "He often knows without being told that something serious is occurring. He senses things." He caressed his son's head. "It's all right, Isaac. You may sit on my lap until you feel better."

As they walked from the small foyer into the *salon* someone knocked on the door, and Ariel opened it to

Anne-Marie and her mother. "Hello," she said. "Please come in."

Madame Leclerc handed her a bouquet of roses arranged in a small wicker basket. "*Bon Anniversaire,* Ariel."

Ariel inhaled the fragrance of the velvety flowers. "Oh thank you. They're gorgeous."

"How charming you look," Madame Leclerc said. "That is a lovely frock."

"It's a present from my parents," Ariel told her. "I'm glad you like it."

"It is indeed beautiful," Anne-Marie said in her careful English. "But it makes you look much older than thirteen."

"Good," Ariel said. "But Isaac won't talk to me. He acts as if he doesn't even know me."

"He sometimes is that way. Soon he will be himself again," Anne-Marie assured her.

"May I put the flowers on this table?" Madame Leclerc asked Ariel. "Then you will not have to hold them."

Ariel's mother came in to greet the Leclercs. "*Bonsoir.* We are glad you could come."

"Look, Mother. They brought roses."

"How lovely they are." Emilie Marsden bent to sniff the fragrance. "Please come in. Mr. Steiner and Isaac have arrived." She led them into the other room.

Again someone knocked and Ariel's father went to see who it was. Ariel wished that it could be Brother Michael. Three people waited there. Father André and two boys who appeared to be about her own age, or perhaps a bit older.

"Good evening." Ariel's father greeted them.

The priest said, "*Bonsoir,* Mr. Marsden and Ariel. These are my nephews, Jacques and Christophe Vevier." He said Vev-yea.

"Please come in. My wife is inside with our other guests. Come and meet everyone."

The boys lingered with Ariel in the foyer. She saw admiration in their eyes, and a small shiver of pleasure rippled across her shoulders. Both boys were attractive. They resembled each other closely, although one was fair and the other dark. She looked from one to the other and back again.

"We are twins," the dark one said. He spoke with the French accent Ariel found so delightful. "I really am the older, though."

"By ten whole minutes," the blond boy reminded his brother.

"Have you brothers or sisters?" the brunet asked Ariel.

"No. I'm an only." She studied their faces. "Which is which?"

"I am Christophe," the blond boy told her. "My brother is Jacques. When we were in America last year we were called Jack and Chris."

"Where did you go in America?" Ariel asked.

But just then their uncle called them and there was no more time to talk. As Ariel started to follow them, someone else knocked and she opened the door.

"Julian!" Ariel stared at Julian Foster.

"Happy Birthday." Julian embraced her. "I told you we'd meet again, didn't I?"

"Yes. Oh, I'm so glad you're here. When did you come?"

"I arrived today by train. I'm settled at the *Hôtel de la Poste.*"

"We stayed there when we first came."

"I know. The manager asked me to bring this letter which arrived for you today."

Ariel glanced at the envelope. It was another letter from Robin. *I'll have to read it later,* she thought, slipping it into her pocket.

"Come and meet the others." She led Julian into the room where everyone was gathered. "Look who's here," she told her mother.

"Julian. How wonderful to see you again. We hoped you'd get here today."

Ariel thought, *They knew she was coming and they didn't tell me.*

As if her mother knew what Ariel was thinking she said, "We weren't sure she'd arrive in time for tonight. We didn't want you to be disappointed if she didn't get here for your birthday. Please introduce her to the others."

Emilie Marsden vanished into the kitchen. Ariel took Julian around the room, introducing her to the other guests. "This is Isaac," she said. "He and I are friends." But Isaac only clung to his father silently.

Once again Hugh Marsden went to the door, and he returned with a slight young woman who stood as if uncertain of her welcome. She was very slender and her long fair hair was pulled back from her face and caught with a rubber band. Her face looked fresh-scrubbed.

"This is Irina Petrovna," Ariel's father said. "She is our friend from the Soviet Union."

Christophe sounded excited when he said, "I have one of your recordings. It's marvelous. The Bach Flute Sonatas."

She smiled shyly without speaking as she went to sit in a corner of the room.

Then Mr. Steiner said, "Look, Isaac. What do you see?"

Isaac looked toward the door. Emilie Marsden stood there holding a crystal plate. On it a birthday cake blazed with candles.

Isaac reached toward it. "Lights," he said. "Lights."

Ariel saw that the white icing was decorated with pink roses. *They even remembered that,* she thought.

Her mother approached her with the cake. "Happy Birthday, darling. Make a wish and blow out the candles."

Ariel shut her eyes. *I wish . . . I wish that everything would be all right.* She opened her eyes and saw Isaac watching the candle flames.

"Will you help me blow them out, Isaac? If they all go out the first time, I get my wish."

From the safety of his father's lap Isaac leaned forward. He looked at Ariel. "Girl," he said. "Lights."

Together they blew all the candles out.

"How old are you today?" Christophe asked her.

"Thirteen."

"We're ahead of you, then," Jacques told her. "We're nearly fifteen. And I'm more nearly fifteen than he is." He glanced at his brother.

"Not that again," their uncle groaned in mock horror. "After all, fifteen is fifteen, is it not?"

Christophe is the one I like better, Ariel thought. *There's something special about him.* She called across the room to Anne-Marie. "Come eat with us. We can go to the dining room."

"The *sàlle a manger*," Anne-Marie said. She told the twins, "Ariel learns French well, even though she has been here only a few days."

"Not really," Ariel said. "But I want to learn. All of you speak such good English. I'm ashamed that I can't speak your language better. I haven't studied French in school yet. I plan to later."

"We liked America," Christophe said. "At least, we liked what we saw."

"Where were you?" Ariel asked. "You didn't have time to tell me."

"Mainly in the state of New Mexico, but we visited California. It is hard to believe the size of that state, it is so large."

"I know. We live in California."

"*Vraiment?* Do you live near the city of San Francisco?"

"No. That's in the northern part of the state. We live about four hundred miles south, near Los Angeles. Did you like San Francisco? I've been there."

"I liked it," Jacques said. "I like the excitement of great cities. Chris likes smaller places better. What about you, Anne-Marie? Do you like cities?"

"Not very much," Anne-Marie said shyly. "I feel confused by all the people and the noise. I too prefer the quiet of a place like Chartres. Better still, I like the country. I sometimes visit a friend who lives on a farm not far from here."

"In San Francisco there is an amazing bridge," Jacques told them. "It is called the Golden Gate bridge. We drove across it. It is an amazing structure."

Ariel had the feeling that Jacques enjoyed using big words. But she thought he used them well.

Christophe said, "From San Francisco we visited a place called Muir Woods. We saw trees higher than any I had ever imagined. They are ancient. They are called redwoods.

"We drove north then, along a road called the Redwood Highway. From time to time we stopped to get out and walk among the trees. Never have I seen such trees. They seem infinitely wise."

"I feel that way about our oak trees at home," Ariel said.

"Yes?" Christophe looked at her thoughtfully. "One morning very early we walked in a grove of those redwood trees and no one was there but us. I became separated from the others." His voice took on a dreamy quality. Ariel thought he must be reliving the experience of that morning.

"The others were in another part of the forest. I stood alone, looking up into one especially beautiful tree. A fine mist surrounded me. But suddenly a shaft of sunlight illuminated the branches and I heard . . ." He stopped speaking.

Ariel's heart began to pound. "What did you hear?"

He looked down and shrugged. "I do not remember. Birds, I suppose."

Ariel was sure he was not telling them what really happened. *Could he have heard the tree sing? I hope he'll tell me, when we know each other better.*

Then Jacques asked Ariel, "Are you ever homesick for California? Even though I like it very much, I missed France while we were away. One misses one's home."

"Yes," Ariel said slowly, "I get homesick. Especially today. I was going to have a big party. It was all planned. I told Anne-Marie."

"What kind of party?" Christophe sounded curious. "Here in France we observe our birthdays mainly with our families." His dreamy manner had passed.

"We were going to swim in my friend's pool. Then we were going to have supper at my house and listen to music afterward in our patio."

"It must have been a great disappointment then, not to have such a *fête*." Jacques sounded sympathetic.

She looked at the three sitting with her. "It turned out all right," she said. "I've met all of you."

"And you received splendid gifts," Anne-Marie reminded her.

"Yes. Will you excuse me a moment? I'll be right back. I'd like to show you my other gift."

She went up to her room and returned with her mother's drawing of Aidan. "My mother drew this. The boy is a friend I had in England. His name is Aidan. He died while we were in Durham."

The twins and Anne-Marie were quiet, looking at the drawing. Christophe was the first to speak. "Suffering shows in his face. But a kind of peace, as well."

Ariel sighed. "It seems so long ago, and it wasn't, really. You all would have liked him."

"Your mother is a true artist," Anne-Marie said. "Where was your friend when he stood here, beside this great cross?"

"On an island in the North Sea called Lindisfarne. It's a very special place. We were there together, my parents and Aidan and I." Suddenly Ariel felt close to these three people. "I'm glad you're here," she told them.

"We are, too." Christophe paused. Then, lowering his voice he asked, "Do you know what is happening? I imagine that we are all aware of something odd. We know that Uncle André is worried. Have either of you been told what is happening?"

"I have not been told," Anne-Marie said, "although my mother has promised that I will know when it is time."

"I think the time is going to be tonight," Ariel told them. "And now that it's so near, I'm scared."

Emilie Marsden stepped into the room. "Ariel, I'm sorry to interrupt, but Isaac is sleepy. Will you show Mr. Steiner your room? Isaac can rest on your bed." Then she looked at the others. "There's more cake. Who'd like another slice?"

Ariel went to the room where Isaac sat on his father's lap. "I'll show you my room, Mr. Steiner. Isaac can sleep on my bed."

Isaac slid off his father's lap and put his hand into Ariel's. "Girl," he said. "Bed."

Ariel looked at Mr. Steiner in surprise. Isaac had been so distant all evening.

"I told you not to be surprised at anything he does or says," he reminded her. "Now he will go with you quite happily. Or do you want me to go with you also?"

"No, Papa. Girl." Isaac was emphatic.

They went up to Ariel's room together. Ariel helped him take off his shoes and lie down on her bed. She covered him with a light blanket. "Would you like to hold my bear?" She showed him Gladly.

Isaac held out his hands. "Bear," he said.

"His name is Gladly. Can you say Gladly?"

"Bear," Isaac repeated, holding Gladly close.

Ariel sat beside him on the edge of the bed. She saw his eyelids flutter, as if he were sleepy.

"Sing, Girl," he ordered.

She sang softly, the lilting French dancing song she had sung to him in the cathedral crypt. Almost at once he was asleep, his face resting against Gladly. She leaned over the child and kissed his cheek. *I don't ever want anything bad to happen to Isaac,* she thought. And she wondered, *When are they going to tell us?*

Ariel put Robin's letter on her dresser. She took the sanctuary knocker from its box and put it in the pocket of her dress. Brother Michael couldn't be with her, but his gift could be a reminder.

She left her bedroom door open so that the light from the hall could shine in. She didn't want Isaac to waken in the dark and be frightened. She tiptoed from the room.

"Is he asleep?" Mr. Steiner asked when Ariel went to sit beside her mother.

"Yes. He went right to sleep. I left the door open so we can hear him if he wakes up."

"Thank you, Ariel. You are very kind to Isaac."

"I just love him," she said. "I wish he were my little brother."

Someone knocked. Ariel's father said, "I believe our last guest has arrived." He went to the door. Hoping against hope Ariel thought, *Could it be Brother Michael after all?*

But it was not Brother Michael. It was a young man whose hair shone golden in the light.

"Mr. Herauld!" Ariel cried. "Mr. Herauld. Where did you come from?"

19

"Good evening." Mr. Herauld's voice was as Ariel remembered it, deep and resonant. As if at a signal, everyone rose. Slowly, deliberately, he gazed into the eyes of each one. When his eyes met Ariel's she shivered as she had the first time she saw him, and the second time as well.

Then he smiled and it was as if a new light had come on in the room. "Please sit down."

For a while no one spoke. Then Jacques asked, "Who are you? Who are you, really?"

"Jacques, do not be rude." Father André's tone was sharp.

"He does not mean to be rude," Mr. Herauld said, "but he is curious. Look up my name in a good dictionary, Jacques, and you will know what I am."

He is so mysterious, Ariel thought.

"It is now time to discuss the reason we are gathered together in this place," Mr. Herauld said. "You have a common interest, a common concern, and that is why you are here. Similar groups are gathered in places all over the world."

"What interest are you talking about?" Jacques asked.

"Jacques," his uncle said firmly, "just listen, please."

Ariel saw Jacques squirm with impatience.

"Mr. Marsden, you have long been deeply concerned about the accumulation of nuclear weapons. You have been quietly talking with people who are equally concerned. That is true of each of the adults in this room."

Jacques asked, "You know about our parents?"

This time Father André did not stop him.

"Yes. Your father is a nuclear scientist and he is, even at this moment, working to find methods by which nuclear power may be used in peaceful and productive ways."

"How do you know all this?" Jacques challenged Mr. Herauld.

But the young man did not answer. Instead he spoke to Irina Petrovna. "You are here as an artist who can move freely in this area."

"Yes," she answered, "but I am no doubt watched."

"However, you are in this room as an assurance that many of your people, too, are concerned."

"Oh yes. We are not all the enemy, although others may think that. Many of my countrymen also long for peace."

"And would you be tempted to seek a home outside your country, now that you are safely here in France?" Mr. Herauld studied her closely.

"No. Never. I am a Russian. My father is a respected member of the Politburo. I would do nothing to bring him harm or shame. I love my father. I love my country." She paused before she said, "There is something I wish I could tell you. If only I knew surely that I can trust you."

"Irina," Mr. Herauld said firmly, "anything you wish to say in secret will remain in this room. No one will disclose any of it. We promise."

Irina Petrovna drew a deep breath. "Then I shall tell you. For some time tensions have existed among the political leaders of my country. At the moment, those who are rigid, who think that war is the only answer, are in power. But my father and some of the others feel very differently. They wage a private, underground

campaign toward peace, toward human rights. It is
dangerous for them. I fear for my father's life. But he
is determined that soon the peace-lovers will come into
power. Then world peace will be a real possibility. And
freedom for the oppressed." She sighed. "If only he will
be in time. If only he could exert some real influence
at the summit meeting."

"Yes." Mr. Herauld's tone was gentle. "And you,
Aaron Steiner. You represent those who are persecut-
ed through the ages. Still, you burn with a desire for
peace and brotherhood."

Isaac's father looked at Mr. Herauld without speaking.

"Julian, you are a healer of bodies. But I think you
are also a healer of souls. You have inherited not only
the name of the one for whom you were named, the
other Julian of Norwich, but you have some of her
spirit as well. She believed that eventually all things
will be well. You believe that, too?"

Julian nodded. "Yes. Dame Julian said that *all
things shall be well, and all things shall be well, and
all manner of things shall be well.* I believe she was
right."

"Even when it doesn't look that way?" Jacques challenged her.

"Even then."

"And Alix," he looked at Anne-Marie's mother, "you
see the cathedral as a possible haven in case of catastrophe. As Noah used his ark, so you would use the
cathedral."

Ariel remembered that when she had first seen it,
the cathedral reminded her of a great stone ship.

"Father André, you have generously made all the
arrangements for this meeting, just as Brother Michael is caring for his group at Durham. Now," he
looked at the young people, "we must know how the

children feel. Which of you will speak for the children of the world?"

No one answered.

"For the children in this room?"

Still no answer.

"For yourself?"

Christophe said, "We simply must not have a nuclear war. It could be the end of everything."

Jacques said, "Little brother, you are such an optimist. It's inevitable. The weapons are stockpiled. People don't build weapons if they don't plan to use them."

"But somehow the use of them could be stopped if enough people cared. Is that not true?" Anne-Marie pleaded with Jacques. "I have never understood the reason for wars. Surely people can learn to live in peace together if they really want to?"

"You are an infant." Jacques' tone was scornful. "A naive infant."

Anne-Marie blushed and looked hurt.

Ariel said, "Don't be mean to her. That's the way wars start. My father thinks that children could do something. So does Mr. Allison, our minister at home. He says that prayers help. I'm sure he's right, but I'm still scared. Mr. Herauld, will there really be a war?"

"That is in the hands of human beings," Mr. Herauld said. "The choice is theirs. The time is growing short."

"I know how true that is." Irina Petrovna spoke so softly that Ariel had to strain to hear her. "My people think that others threaten and challenge them, and they are uneasy. More so each day."

"And we think the same about you . . . about them," Emilie Marsden said. "No one trusts anyone else. It's terrible."

Ariel's father asked, "Mr. Herauld, you must have something in mind. Some way in which we can make a difference. Please tell us what we must do."

"I will tell you only what will happen if you do nothing. Darkness will cover the earth, and who knows when light will shine again?"

Ariel shivered at the bleakness in his words.

"What kind of darkness?" Jacques asked.

"You know, Jack," Christophe answered. "The long winter that scientists like Carl Sagan talk about. Radioactive clouds will come between earth and the sun and nothing will be able to grow. Is that what you mean, Mr. Herauld?"

"Partly. But there are other kinds of darkness. There is also the darkness of the human spirit."

"Yes." Aaron Steiner's tone was bitter. "The kind of darkness which surrounded Hitler, and into which he led my people and destroyed them."

"Stalin too," the Russian woman said. "Much of the time I think all my people live in darkness. Only music makes it possible for me to survive. Music and the friendship of people who think as I do. Musicians and poets and artists all over the world are brothers and sisters. Not enemies."

Julian's soft voice added, "And we must hope and pray that brotherhood and sisterhood among those who work for good, for peace, will be stronger than the forces of darkness."

"Julian," Ariel said, "you're a nurse. What's radiation sickness like?"

Julian looked grave. "It is terrible. It affects the blood, the bone marrow, the entire body."

"I wonder if Aidan died of something like that," Ariel said thoughtfully. "Not radiation, of course. But he told me he thought he could get well if so many terrible things weren't happening."

"It's an interesting thought," Julian said. "The relationship of our bodies to our minds, to our emotions, is a fascinating problem. Aidan was very sensitive to everything around him. No doubt he had a real physical illness, but he may also have been responding to the many faces of darkness."

"We Americans are not exempt," Hugh Marsden said. "We have certainly contributed to the darkness. I think of unspeakable things we have done. Of children burned. Of people homeless."

Ariel remembered the look in her mother's eyes that last day at home when they had sat together. She could hear her mother's voice saying, *I can't stand it when the children are hurt. When the innocent ones have to suffer.*

And her father's voice answering, *It's always the innocent who pay the greatest price.*

"Papa? Girl?" Isaac's voice came to them from the top of the stairs. Aaron hurried to his son and brought him into the room. Sleepily, Isaac clutched Gladly.

Mr. Herauld went to stand by Isaac, gently touching the child's head.

"Light," Isaac said, looking at him. "Light."

Mr. Herauld said, "I must leave you now for a time. Meanwhile, watch for signs. Listen to your own thoughts, your own hearts. Trust your inner voices. You will devise a way to act."

Hugh Marsden went to the door with him, and Ariel thought that the light left with Mr. Herauld.

When Ariel's father returned to the room he stood between his wife and daughter, holding their hands. At first no one spoke. Then Jacques said, "This is all very mysterious and none of it makes sense. What are we supposed to do? I don't understand any of it."

"It is mysterious," Father André said. "But one thing is clear. We are in danger. The entire planet is in danger, and all its people. I know only one solution at a time like this, and that is prayer."

"That's fine, Uncle," Jacques said, "but it isn't concrete. It won't stop a worldwide disaster."

"How can we know that?" Christophe asked his brother. "How can you be so sure?"

"Oh, Chris, you are so naive." Jacques sounded scornful. "You are unrealistic. We live in a world where horrendous things happen, and no one can stop them."

"It is true," Father André said, "that horrendous things happen in the world. What we must not forget is that we, as God's people in the world, live in it, to be sure, but not *of* it. We must never forget whom we serve."

Then Aaron Steiner said, "Cosmic matters may be in crisis, but it is time for this one to be in bed. A child's need for sleep does not wait for the universe to settle itself. Give Ariel her bear, son. We must go now."

But Isaac clung to the bear.

"He can take Gladly tonight," Ariel said. "He needs him."

Hugh and Emilie Marsden looked at each other in surprise. Ariel had never been without Gladly, not since they gave him to her nine years ago.

Seeing their expressions, Ariel said again, "Isaac needs him."

Father André said, "No matter what my outspoken, pagan nephew says, may we be silent together for a moment before we leave each other? May each of us pray in his or her own way for guidance and wisdom in this hour?"

In the silence all Ariel could say was *Please, God. Please don't let it happen. Keep us all safe. Keep everyone safe. Especially Isaac.*

Then, breaking the silence, Father André looked at the group around him and said, before he and the twins left, "Peace be with us."

Aaron Steiner echoed in his deep voice, "Shalom."

Ariel shivered. And later, when everyone had gone and she was in bed, she reached for Gladly before she remembered. She got up and found the sanctuary knocker and put it under her pillow. She would read Robin's letter tomorrow.

When her parents came in to wish her good night she asked, "Daddy, do you think there will really be a war? Soon?"

"We hope not. But things look very bad."

"What can we do? What did Mr. Herauld mean?"

"We have to talk about it and think about it," her father said, bending to kiss her. "Right now, though, try to sleep."

"Thanks for a lovely birthday," Ariel told her parents. "It was wonderful, even though the last part has been scary." Then, taking her mother's hand, she asked, "Will I ever have another birthday?"

20

The morning after her birthday Ariel awoke and reached for Gladly. Then she remembered. She had given him to Isaac. No. She had *loaned* him to Isaac. She reached for the sanctuary knocker under her pillow.

Oh, Brother Michael, she thought, *I wish you were here to tell us what to do. We're all afraid, even my parents. That's really scary.* She held the small bronze knocker so tightly that it cut into her hand.

Finally she laid it on the pillow beside her, got up, found Robin's letter on the dresser, and took it back to bed to read it.

"Dear Ariel,

"I'm really scared. I wish you were here. Ned is sure there's going to be a war soon and he says if there is, nobody will be left alive. I just can't believe it. Can you?

"Anyway, we're leaving here. That's what I wanted to tell you. We're going to stay with my grandparents on their farm in Nebraska, at least for a while. Ned thinks we'd be safer there. He says California would be dangerous in a war because the Russians would aim bombs at the cities. Like Los Angeles. Nebraska would be safer. Except for Omaha. And we won't be anywhere near there.

"Send my next letter in care of Mr. Homer Wilson, R. R. 2, Box 646, Plattesville, Nebraska 69043. Please write soon, will you? I'm so scared. And I miss you.

"Love, Robin.

"P.S. Their phone number is 1-308-246-1172."

Ariel thought about the letter. *What can I tell her?
I'm just as scared as she is.* She dressed and went downstairs, taking the letter with her. Her parents sat in the
sunny kitchen drinking *café-au-lait.*

"Hello, honey," her father said. "Did you sleep
well?"

"Yes. I didn't even dream." She held out Robin's
letter. "Robin's gone to her grandfather's farm in Nebraska. Will she be safe there?"

Her mother reached for the letter. "May I read it?"

"Sure." Ariel asked her father again, "Will they be
safe in Nebraska? Ned thinks they'll be safer there
than in California."

"I suppose he may be right," her father said thoughtfully. "Ned means that the Los Angeles area is more
likely to be directly in the path of a nuclear explosion
than rural Nebraska. But sooner or later the radiation
would drift to Nebraska, I'm afraid."

"So nobody's really safe?"

"I'm afraid that's right."

Her mother handed her Robin's letter. "Be sure to
answer her right away, won't you? Tell her about
France. About your birthday and your new friends.
Maybe that will help cheer her up." Emilie Marsden
sighed. "I shouldn't tell you what to write. She's your
friend. I just can't help wanting her to be safe and
happy. Wanting all of us to be safe and happy."

Ariel drank her hot chocolate and ate her roll and
jam. Everything tasted good. "It's funny, isn't it?" she
said. "The world may soon come to an end, and we go
right on sleeping and eating as if everything was going
to be all right." She spread more jam on her warm roll.
Then she asked her parents, "How did you sleep?"

"We didn't sleep much," her father admitted. "We
talked most of the night. Father André came back

later, after you were asleep. He was restless, too, so we talked the night away. He wants to meet with us in the cathedral this morning. He has something to show us."

After breakfast they walked to the cathedral. Everything looked normal. The building reached toward Heaven as it always had. Tourists flocked around it, although it seemed to Ariel that there weren't as many today as there had been before. People sat at the sidewalk café across the street as they did summer after summer. Swallows dipped and turned against the blue sky. Everything looked peaceful.

Inside the cathedral Father André waited with Mr. Steiner and Isaac. Isaac held Gladly as if the bear were a baby. As Ariel watched, Isaac kissed Gladly's head.

"Bear," he said, patting Gladly. "Good bear."

Ariel longed to hold Gladly, but she couldn't take him away from Isaac. Again she touched the sanctuary knocker in her pocket.

As they stood together in a little group, Julian and Irina joined them. Then Ariel saw Anne-Marie, Christophe, and Jacques coming toward them.

"Anne-Marie," Father André asked, "will you please tell your mother we are ready now?"

Ready for what? Ariel wondered.

When Anne-Marie and her mother joined them, Father André said, "Let us go. I have the key."

Ariel glanced at the twins and they both smiled at her. The group followed the priest as he led them down into the crypt. Isaac began to whimper, burying his head in his father's shoulder as he had the night before. He held Gladly as if he would never let him go.

"It will be all right, son," Mr. Steiner told him. "Soon we will have some light. Don't be afraid." But the child continued to whimper.

They walked along dark, twisting corridors there far below the cathedral. They passed the altar where the statue of Mary and the baby stood.

"Lady," Isaac said, glancing up.

They went deeper and deeper into the far recesses of the crypt. Ariel held her father's hand and followed the beams from the flashlights which the men carried. The powerful rays cast enough light to see by, but they did not dispel the shadows, the cold, or the musty smell.

I don't like it here, Ariel thought. *I want to go back up where it's light.* Suddenly she was aware that Christophe had stepped up beside her. He took her other hand. He didn't say anything, but Ariel was glad he was there.

At last Father André stopped. "Here we are," he told them. "These are the supplies we have been able to accumulate. We have been planning for months. We hope we have thought of everything."

Ariel looked at stacks of boxes and crates piled against the walls. Some were labeled in French, others in English. Milk, canned meats, crackers, canned fruits, soap. Case after case of water. Sleeping bags. And things she could not identify.

Her father said, "Batteries, candles, matches, flints. Oxygen tanks, first-aid supplies, and medicines. Books. What about a shortwave radio?"

Father André showed him. "It is the most powerful we could obtain. It works quite well, even down here. We have placed an antenna against an outer wall of the cathedral. We have done the best we could. Noah had his animals. We have our flashlights and radios. May God have mercy on us all."

"Mr. Herauld told us to do this," Mr. Steiner said. "But I feel that even he believes it will not be enough. Not if it really happens. We could be sustained for a while, but not perhaps long enough. Still, we do what we can."

Ariel looked at Christophe, trying to see his expression in the shadowy light. But his head was turned away from her.

"It isn't the Ritz," Jacques said, "but it's home. 'Be it ever so humble.' " He peered at Ariel. "That's part of a song we learned in America. Do you know it?"

"Yes," said Ariel. "We learned it in school."

Ariel's mother said, "Listen to our voices. They echo down here. Let's sing. Ariel, start us on something, will you?"

All Ariel could think of just then was "Row Your Boat," and she started singing. Soon they all sang and the round swelled and filled the crypt with the ringing of their voices.

"Row, row, row your boat
Gently down the stream;
Merrily, merrily, merrily, merrily,
Life is but a dream."

Life is but a nightmare, Ariel thought as she sang, *and we aren't exactly merry, either.*

Isaac began to cry. His sobs rose above the singing. His father tried to soothe him.

Soon Father André said, "This is what I wanted to show you. It is not to be discussed above. Not with anyone. Do we all understand that? We are not to talk about it. Is it clear to each of you?"

Everyone nodded. Ariel said, "I know we mustn't talk about it, but why will this be just for us? What about all the other people in Chartres? It's their cathedral more than it is ours. What about them?"

The priest said, "It is admirable that you should think of the others. I know this seems to be unfair. But you will soon find that because of the increasing threat of nuclear war, tourists are already leaving for their homes, although they may not be safe in them. And I have been informed by the authorities that the city of Chartres is to be evacuated in the event of war. The citizens are to be urged to go into the country, farther from the town. Most of them will go. We will not. We will remain here, in the cathedral."

The little group went back the way they had come, up into the light. Ariel blinked, her eyes still full of shadows. Isaac lifted his head from his father's shoulder and began to sing in a high, sweet voice, to no particular tune,
"Row, row, bear, bear
Light, Girl, Lady."
Ariel reached to pat his cheek. "You're sweet, Isaac."
He smiled down at her with his lopsided grin, and continued singing. He held Gladly by one furry paw.

Ariel couldn't help wishing that Isaac would hand her the bear. She was slightly ashamed. *I'm thirteen,* she thought. *Why do I still need my teddy bear? But I do.*

Christophe spoke rather formally to Madame Leclerc and Ariel's parents. "Jacques and I would like Ariel and Anne-Marie to be our guests at lunch. May they go with us, please? We know of an outdoor café by the river where we could have a simple meal."

Madame Leclerc asked her daughter, "Would you like that, *Chèrie?*"

Shyly Anne-Marie said, "Yes, please, *Maman.*"

Not at all shyly Ariel said, "Me too."

"Shall the rest of us meet at our house?" Hugh asked the others.

"Thank you," Alix Leclerc said, "but I must return to work."

"And I must practice," Irina Petrovna added.

"I'll come with you," Julian told Emilie Marsden.

The four young people walked away together. The twins led the girls toward a steep flight of stone steps leading down from the back of the cathedral grounds. Soon they were walking beside the river. The sun was warm. A cool breeze blew from the water and suddenly everything seemed pleasant to Ariel.

They went along together, not talking much, all of them enjoying the freedom of air and light after the confining gloom of the crypt.. They paused to watch a family of waterfowl.

"That's a 'paddlin' of ducks,' " Ariel told them.

"What is this?" Anne-Marie was puzzled. "I do not understand."

"That's what the English call them," Ariel explained. Then, thinking of that day on the River Wear, she sighed.

"That was a pretty deep sigh," Christophe said.

"I was thinking of Durham," Ariel told him, "and of my friend Aidan, who died. One day we took a boat ride on the river and we saw ducks then, too. It was peaceful, just like this. I told Aidan that I wanted to pretend that everything was all right with the world. He told me I couldn't be an ostrich and bury my head. I suppose he was right."

"I suppose." Christophe began to say something else, but Jacques broke in.

"Let's talk about food. Let's go to the café. I'm hungry."

"You're always hungry," his twin told him.

"True. I'm a growing boy. I need my sustenance. Come on, Little Brother. Let's eat."

At the café which the twins had chosen they sat together under a striped umbrella. Ariel felt happy and she tried to keep the feeling. She smiled across the table at Anne-Marie, but the French girl looked serious and she did not return the smile.

Ariel said, "Anne-Marie, you look so grim. I know how you feel. But just for a little while, right now, can't we pretend it's an ordinary day and tomorrow will come and it will be ordinary, too? Please?"

"I will try," Anne-Marie said, "but I think it will not be easy because everything is not all right and we all know it." She turned to Jacques. "What is the oxygen for? All those tanks? Tell us, please, what you know about all those things which are stored in the crypt."

Jacques looked at his brother. Christophe nodded. "Tell them," he said. "Tell them all we know."

Jacques buttered a breadstick and took a bite. "Try one," he said. "They're good. Well, the oxygen is to keep us alive while the crypt is sealed so that radiation won't reach us as soon as it might if we were not sealed in. Is that much clear?"

Ariel shuddered. "I hate the thought of being shut up down there. I absolutely hate it."

Christophe reached to pat her hand.

"Don't treat me like a child," she flared.

He withdrew his hand at once. "I am sorry, Ariel. I touched you only to let you know that I, too, deplore the thought." He looked hurt.

"Oh, Chris," she said, "I'm sorry too. I guess I'm just on edge."

Jacques cleared his throat. "To continue," he said, holding up his gnawed breadstick as if it were a baton, "we won't use the oxygen tanks while there's still enough natural air in the crypt. Oh happy thought." He grinned at Ariel. "But if we didn't have medical oxygen to use, sooner or later . . . mostly sooner . . . we'd all die from carbon monoxide poisoning. Oh unhappy thought." This time he grinned at Anne-Marie.

"How can you joke about these horrible things?" Anne-Marie's cheeks were flushed. "I do not understand how you can joke when it is our very lives you are talking about."

Jacques looked at her. Then he said gently, "Surely you know that I am only whistling in the dark, as they say in America. To keep up my courage. It frightens me, too."

Anne-Marie looked at Ariel. "Now we are even," she said with a sad little smile. "I, too, am sorry. I lost my temper. Please tell us more, Jacques. I'll be quiet."

"It's all right, *Chèrie*," he said. "I know how you feel.

At any rate, when the oxygen in the tanks is all used up, we hope it may be safe to let in some air from the outside. We hope the radiation level may have dropped by that time."

"How will we know when we're running out of oxygen?" Ariel asked. "That scares me. It all scares me."

Jacques took a bite of his cherry yogurt. "Good question, my dear. Candles begin to flicker when there isn't enough oxygen. We're counting on being able to let in air from outside. We have a device for measuring radiation levels, you understand. But our father thinks . . ."

Christophe stopped him. "Jack!"

"I don't care. We're all old enough to cope. We'll have to, anyway."

"What were you going to say, Jacques?" Anne-Marie insisted. "What about your father?"

Jacques looked at his brother who shrugged in that very French way.

Jacques told them, "As you know, our father is a nuclear scientist and he and Mother are in New Mexico. Father is involved in a very confidential project just now. Mr. Herauld came to talk to them. Right after that Father sent us here to be with Uncle André.

"Father says that the whole earth is doomed if there is a full-scale nuclear war. He says that none of us will survive because the whole atmosphere will change. Light will not be able to penetrate the cloud of soot and dust which will form between earth and the sun. Everything will be dark and cold and nothing will grow. No crops, no livestock. No us."

The four young people were silent, each with private thoughts. Jacques spoke again. "If it really happens, we're all doomed. We could probably survive for a while down there in the crypt. But I think, my father thinks, people like Carl Sagan think that it would be the end of everything."

"How can we let it happen?" Ariel was angry. "Can't somebody stop it? What good are all the secret meetings? Why did we have to come here if we're going to die anyway?"

"I have asked myself these same questions," Anne-Marie said. "But I have no answers, either."

"When did it all start?" Jacques turned to his twin. "How long ago was it? And *how* did it start?"

Christophe did not answer, but he asked Ariel, "When did it start for you? When did you first find out that something strange was happening? Can you remember?"

21

"Of course I remember," Ariel said. "It was the day Mr. Herauld came to my house. I remember because that was the day Robin and I were talking about my birthday party out by the pool, and when I got home I found out that there wasn't going to be any party."

"But when was it exactly?" Jacques asked. "I don't suppose you remember the date, do you?"

Ariel thought. "Well, it was five weeks ago because I remember Robin asked me how we were possibly going to wait five weeks till my birthday."

"And when you got home that day, Mr. Herauld was there?"

"Yes. He was coming out of my house. He had already talked to my parents." Ariel remembered her dream, too, but she did not mention it.

Christophe said to Jacques, "Five weeks ago. That is just about when he talked to our parents in New Mexico, wasn't it?"

"No. It can't have been that long ago." Jacques tilted back in his chair and lazily brushed away a fly that circled him.

"I'm sure it was, Jack. Remember . . ."

Anne-Marie interrupted him. "I remember exactly when I first saw him. It was at our home here in Chartres and it was the second of June."

"How can you remember the exact date?" Jacques asked her.

"Because it was my birthday."

"You both have birthdays to remind you. Well, this didn't begin on our birthday." Jacques asked his brother, "How can we recall an exact date?"

"My diary," Christophe said. "We can check it in my diary."

"Let's go." Jacques suddenly shoved his chair back from the table. The dishes and silver clattered. "Chris, that's a wonderful idea." He grinned at Anne-Marie. "My little brother keeps a journal. He writes all his deep thoughts and every earth-shattering event and all his secret longings and loves."

"Jack," Christophe scowled at his twin. "I've warned you!"

Jacques shrank back from Christophe in mock terror, shielding his face with his hands. "Peace. Peace. I've never looked inside the covers of your sacred book. I promised. But let's go."

The boys paid the bill and the four of them left the café, hurrying toward the house where the twins lived with their uncle.

"Not so fast," Ariel gasped. "These cobblestones hurt my feet. Do we have to run?"

Christophe took her hand and pulled her along uphill toward the house near the cathedral. Hot and out of breath, they ran into the living room. Anne-Marie collapsed on the sofa, but Ariel was too excited to sit down.

"Excuse me, please," Christophe said, "I'll be right back."

"Hurry, Chris," Jacques called as he stood over Anne-Marie, fanning her hot face with a magazine.

Ariel looked around impatiently. Bookcases lined two walls of the room. A large globe of the world stood in a corner. From the windows she could see the cathedral spires.

Christophe came back into the room slowly, reading

as he walked. He looked up to stare at his brother. "I was right, Jacques. But look at this." He held the diary out to Jacques, pointing to an entry.

"It can't be," Jacques said. "You must have made a mistake."

"It's not a mistake." Christophe turned to Anne-Marie. "You said that Mr. Herauld came here to Chartres on the second of June?"

"Yes. It was the second."

"Do you remember what time it was?"

Anne-Marie thought for a moment. "It was at about eight-thirty in the evening. Mr. Steiner and Isaac and your uncle had dined with us. We had finished the meal and we were talking together when someone knocked at the door. *Maman* went, and when she came back, Mr. Herauld was with her."

"It is not possible," Christophe said. "He was with us on June second at four in the afternoon. But he could not have done it. Not even on the Concorde." He stood there shaking his head. Then he asked, "Ariel, can you remember what date it was when he came to your home in California?"

"It was a Friday afternoon five weeks ago. I don't remember the date, but I remember the time." She remembered all of it. "He went to Aidan's house in Ohio, too. He told me. That same afternoon. And I have to tell you something else. The night before he came, Aidan and I each had a dream. The same dream."

The twins and Anne-Marie looked at Ariel as if they could not believe what she was telling them.

"Well, I can't help it," she said defiantly. "It's true. We both dreamed that . . ."

"Your homes were destroyed," Christophe interrupted.

"And Mr. Herauld came and told you not to be afraid." Anne-Marie was breathless. "*Oh Ciel* ! What is happening to us?"

"We thought it was because we were twins," Jacques said. "It happened to us once or twice before, when we were much younger, that we dreamed the same dream. We just took it for granted. But this time it was so vivid. So real." He looked at his brother. "Chris, what would the date be, five weeks ago yesterday on a Friday?"

Christophe checked his diary. "June second. What time was it, Ariel?"

"It was about four in the afternoon. I remember because I asked Robin what time it was. She said it was ten to four and it takes me about ten minutes to ride my bike home from her house."

They looked at each other. Jacques was the first to speak. "But it isn't possible. Not even with the time changes. No one on earth could do it."

"No one on *earth*." Ariel spoke softly.

Jacques stared at her as if she were out of her mind. "What are you saying?"

All four were silent. Ariel was conscious of a clock ticking somewhere, of a bee buzzing against the windowpane. Of her heart thudding, and of her own breathing. Then she asked, "Do you have a dictionary? He told Jacques to look up the name Herauld."

Jacques took a large dictionary from the bookcase. "Herauld isn't here," he said in a moment, "but *herald* is. It comes from an old French word, *herau(l)t* which means *Messenger*."

When no one spoke, Jacques shook his head. "But this is the twentieth century. The last part of the twentieth century, not the Middle Ages. Such things just do not happen anymore. If they ever did."

Anne-Marie asked, "Does it really matter what century this is? We all know that Mr. Herauld is not like any of us."

"And he sort of shines," Ariel said. "Even Isaac noticed it."

"Especially Isaac," Anne-Marie agreed.

Christophe said, as if he were talking to himself, "Could it be possible? Could he be . . ."

"What are you suggesting?" Jacques sounded angry and impatient. "That he's from another planet? That he's some kind of angel? I don't believe any of this. It's all crazy. Anyway, if he's that weird, he should call in the rest of his troops."

Ariel was surprised at the severity in Anne-Marie's tone when she reproved Jacques. "I do not like it that you always joke, even about the most serious things. You say it is because you are frightened. But can you never be serious?"

"And can you never be a little more relaxed?" Jacques countered. "It does no good to be so solemn all the time. You are always tense. You never smile. You make me uncomfortable."

Anne-Marie looked down. Ariel saw a blush rise and tint her cheeks. Ariel hoped that Anne-Marie wouldn't cry. Not in front of Jacques.

"Jacques, there's no need to be rude." Christophe frowned at his twin.

"You are right again." Jacques stood and bowed deeply to Anne-Marie. He took her hand and kissed it before she could snatch it away. "Many pardons, *Mademoiselle*. You are *tout-à-fait charmante*. Altogether charming. And you have stolen my heart."

"And you are *tout-à-fait impossible*," Anne-Marie answered.

But Ariel thought she saw the flicker of a smile on the French girl's lips.

"In any case," Christophe said, "I wonder if we will see Mr. Herauld again."

"He said we would," Ariel reminded Christophe. "And he told us to watch for signs."

Jacques went to the window and looked up. "Behold, I watch," he said. Then he turned toward Anne-Marie and fell to his knees, putting his hand over his heart. "Won't you watch with me?" he begged.

"You're a clown, Jacques," Ariel laughed. And for a moment the tension was broken.

22

Anne-Marie smiled at Jacques, a warm smile that made her eyes shine. "It is difficult to remain cross with you," she said. "You are so absurd. Thank you, but I must go home now."

"And you have those errands to do for Uncle," Christophe reminded his brother.

"*Oui*. But first I shall walk with Anne-Marie to the cathedral. *Adieu*."

"Thank you both for lunch," Ariel called after Jacques. She wished that she could spend some time with Christophe alone.

As if he had been thinking the same thing, he said, "There is something I would like to show you. Will you go with me?"

"I'd like to, but I'd better check with my parents."

"A good idea." Christophe picked up a long, narrow black leather case, and they went toward Ariel's house. Inside, her parents were talking with Julian.

"Did you have a nice lunch?" her mother asked.

Ariel glanced at Christophe. "Yes. It was super. We ate outside by the river."

Christophe asked Hugh Marsden, "Sir, may I have your permission to walk with Ariel for a while now?"

He's so polite, Ariel thought. *I can't imagine Kevin talking that way.*

"Certainly, if Ariel would like to." Ariel's father looked at her questioningly.

She nodded.

"Can you be back by four-thirty?" her mother asked.

"I'll have her back by then," Christophe assured Ariel's mother.

As Ariel and Christophe walked back toward the cathedral Ariel saw Mr. Steiner and Isaac coming out. Isaac held Gladly as he had before, like a baby in his arms.

When he saw Ariel he waved the bear, holding it by one stubby leg. "Girl. Bear." He ran to her.

She stopped to hug the little boy, but when she reached for Gladly, Isaac ran away from her. "Mine," he said. "Mine bear."

"The bear is not yours, Isaac," Mr. Steiner said. "He belongs to Ariel. Remember? She has been kind enough to lend it to you. It is Ariel's bear, not yours. But we will get you a bear of your own."

Isaac only clung to Gladly and repeated, "Mine bear."

He really believes Gladly is his, Ariel thought. *How am I going to persuade him to give him back?*

Abruptly Isaac ran toward the statue on the column, Ariel's Princess Emilie. "Lady," he said, "see." He held Gladly up as high as he could reach. "Mine bear." Then he ran away again, laughing. His father hurried to catch him.

"Well, good-bye, everyone," Ariel said. "I'll see you later."

Christophe and Ariel walked down the steps behind the cathedral, toward the river. The sun was warm, the summer afternoon quiet and bright.

"Why can't it stay this way?" Ariel asked. "Why can't it stay peaceful? Let's pretend that we're just here on a vacation and pretty soon we'll go home again and everything will be the same as it was."

Christophe glanced at Ariel. "You're having a pretty hard time accepting all of this, aren't you?"

"I guess so," Ariel admitted. "Aidan told me that I shouldn't try to hide from it. He said I have to face it, whatever it is. But I don't want to. Not yet."

"I understand. But Ariel, look." He stopped before a corner kiosk where newspapers were sold. "Can you read the headlines?"

"No," she said, glancing at the papers, "and I don't want to know what they say."

"Oh Ariel, you must open your eyes. You must."

"I will. But later. Not now." Desperately she changed the subject. "What's in your case?"

"I'll show you later."

"Where are we going?"

"Just to walk along the river. Jacques and I discovered a spot one day. I'd like to show it to you."

"Do you like being a twin?"

"Yes. Jacques and I are very close. Closer, I believe, than brothers who are not twins."

"You're different from each other," Ariel said.

"I know. Still, we are close. And you? You are an only child?"

"Yes. Sometimes I wish I had a brother or a sister. And sometimes I like it just the way it is. I guess I'm used to having our family a threesome."

"Threesome?" Christophe tried the word as if it were unfamiliar to him. "I have not heard this expression before. If your family is a threesome, are you and I a twosome?"

Ariel laughed. "At home we say that when two people are dating."

"I see." He was quiet for a moment. Then he asked, "But cannot we be a twosome just now, while we are walking together? I like the word."

"I don't see why not." Ariel liked the word, too, and the feeling it gave her here with Christophe.

They walked past small shops and houses. Everything looked serene—flowers in gardens, children playing ball. She thought, *Surely nothing can be wrong when everything looks just the way it does at home. Quiet and ordinary.*

Soon they came to a park where a wide expanse of green was still damp from a morning watering. "Doesn't it smell good?" Ariel sniffed the air.

"Yes. I like the fresh smell, as if it had been raining."

They crossed a stone bridge, pausing to look down at the river flowing calmly below them. Christophe led Ariel to a clump of willow trees. Hidden behind them, scarcely showing at all, was a bench. When they sat on it Ariel felt as if she were looking through a soft green curtain.

"It's beautiful," she said. "It's like a cave, sort of. We can hide here." Through the mesh of willow branches she saw the river, waterfowl, trees dipping their branches into the water. She saw no other people.

"I love it," she said to Christophe. "It's perfect. These are weeping willow trees, aren't they? We have them at home."

"Yes. I especially like them." ·

Ariel wondered whether Christophe would tell her about his special tree. She asked him, "What are your favorite trees?"

Without hesitation he said, "The California redwoods. And yours?"

"California oaks. There's an enormous one in front of our house. It's my favorite tree in the whole world."

Christophe nodded, but he said nothing more about trees. He opened his case and silver flashed in the sunlight.

"A flute!" Ariel said. "It's my favorite instrument."

Christophe assembled the flute and tentatively blew a few breathy sounds. Then he played some rapid scales. And then he played something which Ariel had never heard before. It was not exactly a song, or a dance, and she did not recognize the melody.

The tones floated above them, tangled in each other, and mingled with the breeze, the river, and the willows. Ariel was caught in a moment full of light and sound and she wanted it to go on forever.

When Christophe finished playing, she realized that she was holding her breath. She let it out softly and began to breathe again. Then, on impulse, she sang back to Chris his winding, floating melody. He began to play again and the tones of his flute mingled with the sound of her voice. She continued to feel that everything was perfect—the music, the river, the sun, Christophe, and herself.

When their music stopped, Christophe looked at Ariel in astonishment. "How did you do that?" he asked. "I don't understand. I have not played that for anyone until now. It is something that has been in my head for a long time, a kind of musical secret I have with myself. Yet you heard it only once and sang it back to me. I simply do not understand."

Ariel looked at the ground. She studied it as if it were important, moving her foot back and forth as if to feel the texture of the grass.

"Ariel?" Christophe persisted. "How do you do it?"

"It's just something I've always been able to do," she told him. "When I hear a piece of music that I really like, it stays in my head and I remember it and then I can sing it back. It's just the way it is. And what you played . . . well, I love it. It makes me think of the river and the way it flows and sparkles in the sun. I just wanted to sing it."

Christophe nodded. Then he said, "Only once in my life have I heard music so completely beautiful as your voice sounded just now. Only once."

23

"Was it in California?" Ariel asked Christophe. "Was it a redwood tree?"

He looked at her and she felt that he trusted her completely. "Yes. And you have heard a tree singing, too." It was not a question.

"Yes." *That makes four of us,* Ariel thought. *Brother Michael and Aidan and I. And now Christophe.*

She glanced at him. Light glinted from the silver flute. Sun filtered through the willow branches. She was sure that Christophe stared far off into a distant time as he remembered a distant music.

"Will you tell me, please?" she asked him.

"Yes. I want to tell you," Christophe said to her. "At first I thought I was dreaming. It was as if I were alone in the forest with the trees. Sunlight slanted from them and I looked up to try to see their tops. They are incredibly high. Suddenly one of them began to sing. It was . . . I need not tell you, for you have heard it, too. Will you please tell me about the time you heard it?"

"I've heard it more than once," she told him. "When I was little, my oak tree used to sing often. I wasn't even surprised the first time I heard it. Then it stopped. But I heard a tree sing on the island of Lindisfarne. And a tree sang outside the cathedral at Durham."

"Do you know anyone else who has heard them sing? Anyone besides you and me?" Christophe asked.

"Yes. Two others. Aidan heard the tree on Lindis-

farne. And just before he died he heard the tree near
the cathedral at Durham. And Brother Michael has
heard the music, too. I asked him."

"Who is this Brother Michael?"

"He's a monk," Ariel told him. "He lives in Durham.
He gave me this." She showed him the sanctuary
knocker.

Christophe studied it. "What a fierce-looking lion."

"Yes. I touch him when I'm trying to be brave." She
laughed at herself. "I seem to touch it a lot."

"I can understand why," Christophe said. Suddenly
his speech sounded very French, although he spoke in
English. "And what do you think it means, this singing
of the trees?"

Ariel spoke slowly, searching for the right words.
She felt sure that Christophe would understand what
she said about it, but she wanted to make it clear to
herself as well as to him.

"At first I didn't even think about it," she said.
"When I was little I'd just listen to the tree when it
sang. It seemed so natural. I'd be sitting up there in the
branches looking at the sky, listening to the birds, and
it would start to sing.

"Sometimes I'd sing with it. Sometimes I'd just listen. I never wondered what was happening. It just happened." She tried to remember exactly how it had been.
"And then for a long time it didn't sing again. I don't
know why. Maybe I forgot to listen for it. But when I
really wanted to hear it sing again, before we left home,
it didn't. I think Mr. Herauld knew. He didn't say anything, but I think he knew."

Christophe focused all his attention on Ariel, listening to every word. It seemed to her that he wanted to
hear even the things she didn't say. "And then?" he
asked her. "When did you hear the singing again?"

"When Aidan and I were with my parents on Lindisfarne. Have you been there?"

"No, but I have often thought that I would like to go there one day. Please tell me about the tree on Lindisfarne."

"Well, Aidan and I were standing there under the tree, near a big Celtic cross, and the wind was cold. It's on the North Sea, you know. All of a sudden the tree began to sing. That's all. It just began to sing. And we both heard it."

"Do you think your parents heard it, too?"

"No. And I've never told them about it. I haven't told Robin, either."

"I'm glad you told me. The Lindisfarne tree is the one in your mother's drawing of your friend Aidan, isn't it?"

"Yes."

"And then? The tree at Durham?"

"It was the night Aidan died. I had been asleep. I dreamed that someone was singing. Then I woke up and I still heard singing, and it was the tree."

Thinking about that night, speaking about it, Ariel was thrown back into the old familiar grief.

"You are still sad." Christophe sounded concerned. "It was a very short time ago. Maybe it is still too soon for you to talk about it."

"I want to tell you. You see, I've never understood any words when the trees sang. But that night when Aidan heard the tree sing, I think he understood the words. He was going to tell me, but he died before he could." Ariel felt tears slide down her cheeks. "I sang at his funeral. One of the monks played his flute while I sang 'The Lord's My Shepherd.' "

Christophe leaned to wipe away her tears with his fingers. His touch was gentle and she thought he knew exactly how she felt.

"I did not understand the words, either, when the redwood tree sang," he said. "But I am sure of something. I am sure it sang out of joy. Pure joy. It could only be for joy that such music could be sung. We cannot understand it because we have never been happy in that same way."

Ariel remembered the smile on Aidan's face at the very moment of his death. "Aidan was that happy," she told Christophe. "He saw something that made him happy, just before he died. He knew something and he couldn't tell us. He didn't have time."

"Time," Christophe said thoughtfully. "Do you realize that's what we are running out of if we are actually living our last days right now? There will not be time for me to become . . . what I want to be. Or for you to become a singer. Or for Jacques to learn to stop hiding behind jokes. Or for serious Anne-Marie to discover the joy of laughter. But I cannot believe . . ." He stopped speaking and looked out across the river.

"What, Chris?"

He looked at her. "You called me Chris. I like it. They called me that in America."

"What can't you believe?" Ariel persisted.

"I cannot believe that it will really happen. There must be a way to stop it. To make sure that it never happens."

Ariel said, "I always thought I'd grow up. I just took it for granted. But now? I'm only thirteen. I'm not ready for the world to stop."

Christophe laid his hand on hers and she was comforted by his touch. "Chris?"

"Yes?"

"I'm reading a book that's partly about dying," she told him. "*A Ring Of Endless Light.* And it's about right now. I mean about people as young as we are who are living right now. The girl's name is Vicky. Her grandfather's a minister. He's sick and he knows he's going to die pretty soon. And he's happy about it. Really happy. He keeps telling his family that the next life is going to be absolutely wonderful. He's really looking forward to dying, that's how sure he is."

"But if he's a grandfather, he's old, is he not? And this Vicky. How does she feel about it?"

"She loves her grandfather. He's one of her favorite people and she doesn't want him to die. She's sort of like us. Wondering what it would be like. She doesn't die, but other people do, in that book."

"Then it is a sad book?"

"No. That's the funny thing. It's a happy book. I wish my best friend could read it. Robin. I wish you could meet her. I had a letter from her and I haven't answered it yet. She's gone to live on her grandparents' farm in Nebraska and she's scared, too, because of what's happening."

Ariel felt suddenly that she had to write to Robin. She wished she could see her, talk to her. "Chris," she said, "I've got to write to her right away. Can we go back now?"

"Yes. It is time we started back." As he put the flute away in its case he suggested, "Why don't you telephone your friend? We talk to our parents in New Mexico quite often. We call at eight in the evening and it is noon there. Would it not please you to talk to her?"

"Oh yes, I never thought of that. I'll ask my father if I can call her tonight."

They walked back the way they had come. When they reached the newspaper stand Ariel stopped and looked at a paper. "Chris," she asked, "what do the papers say?"

"Are you sure you want to know?"

"Yes."

"They speak of tension between super-powers. They say that the Soviet Union is accusing NATO of an arms buildup. They question the effectiveness of the September summit meeting."

"Do you think it will happen?" she asked him. "Do you think there really will be a war?"

"Who knows?" Chris was thoughtful as they strolled along together. "It seems more and more likely. But at the moment I would like to think only about the pleasure of this afternoon, not of the dark things. I wish to think of music and sunlight and friendship."

Ariel smiled at him. "You sound like me now. Putting off thinking about the bad things until later."

"I know." When they reached the ancient half-timbered house which was Ariel's temporary home Chris said, "Thank you for a most pleasant time."

In spite of herself Ariel laughed.

"Why do you laugh?" He looked surprised.

"I'm not laughing at you," she said quickly. "Really I'm not. I was just thinking how different you are from a boy I know at home."

"Are you and he a *twosome?*" Chris pronounced the word carefully.

"No." She was glad she could say it. "No, we aren't."

"Bien," Chris said. "Good." He brushed her nose lightly with his finger. "I like your cinnamon freckles. And I like your hair when the sun shines on it. I'm glad you are so natural. You are very sweet."

Ariel felt a glow of happiness. He liked her, straight hair, freckles, and all. "Thank you," she said softly.

Chris smiled at her. *"À bientôt,"* he said. "That means until the happy time when we meet again."

"See you later," she called, as he walked away. She was surprised at how happy she felt, in spite of everything.

24

That night Ariel spoke to Robin on the telephone. "Hello, Robin. It's me, Ariel."

"Ariel! But you're in France."

"I know. And you're in Nebraska."

"I don't believe this." Ariel heard Robin's familiar laugh. "It's really you."

"How are you?" In spite of the time apart from Robin and the miles between them, Ariel felt that the separation didn't matter. They could have been in their own homes in California, calling each other as they often did in the evening. Yet something was different.

Robin said, "I'm OK, I guess. How are you?"

"OK. But I miss you."

"Me too. How do you like France?"

"I like it. How do you like Nebraska? Is it fun on a farm?"

"It's OK. But it's hot and dusty and I sneeze a lot."

"I got your letter," Ariel told her. "It came on my birthday."

"Did you have a party?"

"Sort of." Ariel wanted to be able to tell Robin about her new friends, about Mr. Herauld, but she knew there wasn't time. She asked Robin, "Are you really all right?"

"I guess so." Robin's voice sounded shaky. "Ned is sure that there is going to be a war. I'm awfully scared.

I think my mother and my grandparents are, too, but they try to hide it."

"I know what you mean."

A silence stretched between the girls. Then Ariel said, "I've met a really nice boy. Chris. He plays the flute. He's fifteen. You'd like him."

"What does he look like?" Robin asked.

"He's blond." Ariel knew that didn't say much about Christophe. She looked at her watch. "My time is almost up. I just wanted to talk to you."

"I'm glad you called. How's your father? And your mother?"

"Fine. Robin?"

"What?"

"You're still my best friend."

"You're mine, too."

"Well, good-bye." Ariel wanted to say much more. She wanted to be able to tell Robin about the crypt, about all the things she was afraid of. But she couldn't. There wasn't time. What she really wanted was to be with Robin and talk the way they always had.

"Listen," Robin said, "I'm glad you called. I wanted to tell you about something. At the church we go to there's a deep cellar underneath. They have tornadoes here, you know. And they've got this cellar fixed up like a kind of bomb shelter. We practice going into it sometimes, even at night. It's really scary."

Ariel felt her heart begin to beat faster. "I know what you mean," she said, thinking about the crypt.

"And there's something else." Robin hesitated.

"What?"

"I think we're going to have to use it. Before we left home I had a dream. It was terrible. It was so real. I think we'll really have to use the cellar."

"Oh, Robin," Ariel said to her friend, "I had a dream, too. I know what you're saying."

"You do? You mean you think it was the same dream?"

"Maybe. Probably."

"That's weird," Robin said. "Well, anyway, I'm glad you called."

"Listen, Robin," Ariel said in a rush. "Please keep believing that something good will happen. Try to believe there won't be a war. Will you try? It's important."

"Sure. That's what I want to believe."

When she had hung up, Ariel sat staring at the phone as if Robin might materialize somehow. She felt as if the conversation wasn't finished. And she wondered if she'd ever hear Robin's voice again.

"Was it a good connection?" Her father came into the room.

"Yes. It was just like it is at home."

"How is Robin?"

"She's OK. Well, not really. She's scared. I wish she could be here with us. At least we'd be together when it happens. If it happens."

Her father put his hand on her shoulder, but he did not speak.

"Thanks for letting me call, Daddy."

"You're welcome." They went to the kitchen together. Ariel asked her parents, "Who is Mr. Herauld really? Do you know? He's somebody strange. We were talking about him today at Father André's house. We went there because Jacques wanted Chris to look up something in his journal. We realized that Mr. Herauld came to all of our houses on the same day. Even Aidan's. And that isn't possible. And even before I met him the first time, that day at our house, I dreamed about him. Maybe I shouldn't tell you this, but they didn't say not to. The twins had the same dream. So did Anne-Marie. And Robin. And Aidan. I don't see how a thing like that can happen. I don't understand it at all.

It scares me. We're all scared and we just can't understand it."

Her mother said, "It is not unheard of for people to dream identical dreams. It does happen. Can you tell us about the dream?"

Ariel felt a little better, just knowing that this kind of thing had happened to other people. Still, her dream . . . their dreams . . . had been terrible. "We dreamed that our homes were ruined. Our trees were all dead. Then Mr. Herauld came and told us not to be afraid. He said he had come to help us. It's all unreal. We just can't see how it's possible."

Her father said, "I know how you must feel. Some things seem to be past belief. But I think we must try to accept such things, when they happen, even though we may not understand them. We twentieth-century people tend to believe only what we can explain, only what we can touch. But that does not mean that we can dismiss things which happen outside our scope of time and place."

"That's pretty involved, Hugh," Emilie Marsden protested.

"I know. At any rate, Ariel, try not to worry. Just accept what happens."

Well, Ariel thought, *whatever happens, at least we don't have secrets from each other anymore.*

25

The Marsdens and Anne-Marie and her mother walked together to the cathedral for the concert. Late evening sunlight touched the ancient stone, gilding even the Princess Emilie's stone gown. Father André, looking preoccupied, the twins, Mr. Steiner, and Julian waited at the west door.

"Where's Isaac?" Ariel asked.

"He is being cared for. He loves music, but his attention span is short and I do not wish him to be a disturbance." Isaac's father smiled at Ariel. "But I thank you for asking about him."

The ten of them went in together and found seats near each other. Ariel sat between Christophe and her mother. Jacques sat beside Anne-Marie. A platform had been put in place for the orchestra and soon they began to come in. Before long the huge nave was full. People sat along the sides, too, behind pillars, on steps, in every available bit of space.

Ariel shivered with pleasure as the orchestra members began tuning their instruments. The sound was exciting, as if it could lead to something wonderful. And it did.

The concert opened with a suite of dances by Bach. The people were so still that only music was heard—no scraping of chairs, no talking, no coughing. Only music.

Next Irina Petrovna took her place in front of the orchestra. She looked small, almost childlike, standing there in her simple white dress, her hair pulled back in its rubber band. But she no longer seemed childlike when she began to play. The silver tones floated up into the vast reaches of the cathedral, up, up, until they seemed to vanish into Heaven. The only light, as darkness fell, came from a floodlight above Irina, touching her fair hair, making the silver flute gleam.

Ariel found her hand held warmly in Christophe's hand and she wanted to stay forever in this safe place, near Chris and her parents, with music all around.

When Irina finished playing Chris said, "She's a great artist. I wish that someday I could . . ."

"Is that what you meant yesterday?" Ariel asked quietly. "When you said that you might not have time to become what you want to be? You want to be a flutist, like her?"

"Yes. It's what I've always wanted to do."

"Maybe it will be all right. Maybe there will be time." Ariel desperately hoped there would be time. For all of them. For everyone.

After the concert Ariel and her parents and friends went to speak to Irina Petrovna. Suddenly Ariel was shy, thinking, *She's famous. Tonight she's different. I wonder if I should speak to her.* Aloud, she asked her mother, "Is it all right to speak to her?"

"I'm sure it is," her mother said.

"She looks worried, doesn't she?" Ariel asked. "And sort of pale."

"Yes, but she's always pale. And maybe it's just the stress of playing in this place before all those people."

So Ariel gathered her courage and said to the flutist, "I loved your music. I wanted it to go on and on."

Irina bent to kiss Ariel on both cheeks. "Thank you. That makes me happy."

Christophe told Irina, "You are a great artist. I wish I could study with you."

"Thank you, Christophe. That is a fine compliment."

At that moment Father André strode toward them looking solemn and grave. He nodded to Irina. "It is true."

Irina took Ariel's hand, as if she needed to touch someone at that moment. "You tell them, please," she said to the priest.

"Come," he said, "please follow me." He led them into a shadowy corner of the building. Ariel pressed close to her parents. Anne-Marie held her mother's hand. Julian stood near Aaron Steiner. The twins stared at their uncle.

Jacques asked, "What's wrong, Uncle André? Is it our parents?"

"No, Jacques. They are all right. I have just spoken with your father. Irina received an urgent message from her father just before she played." He turned to face Irina. "What a difficult time to receive such a message. You played magnificently, despite everything."

"Uncle!" Jacques was impatient.

"Softly, Jacques," Father André said. "We must go directly to the crypt. Aaron, get Isaac as quickly as you can and join us there."

"I'd like to go with you, Aaron," Julian said. "Perhaps I can help."

When they had gone Father André said, "Let us go quickly."

They went into the crypt. By the beams of a flashlight Father André led them deeper and deeper into the darkness. Ariel became aware of silence. None of the noise from above penetrated to these depths. It was as if they were the only people left in the world.

Soon Julian arrived with Aaron Steiner, who carried his sleeping son. Isaac clutched Ariel's bear, even in his sleep. The people in the crypt looked at each other, but no one spoke. Ariel began to shiver, partly with fear, partly with the chill of the place.

"So," Father André said finally. "It has begun. Now, Irina, please tell us of your father's call."

"He warned me that there is grave danger. He did not have time to tell me what the danger is, but he told me to seek a safe place."

"And, boys," Father André said to the twins, "your father called with the same message. He is now on his way to Washington, as are some of the American President's other advisers."

"Then it is truly serious." Ariel's father put one arm around her and the other around his wife, as if he could shelter them both.

"Christophe, please see if you can find us a news report on the radio," Father André said.

Static and a jumble of voices were all Ariel heard at first. Then, quite clearly, came a man's voice, speaking in French. Ariel could not understand the words, but she heard the tension in the voice.

When he had stopped speaking Alix Leclerc said, "*Oh Ciel!*"

"Please translate for the others, Christophe," his uncle told him.

Christophe was suddenly pale as he told them, "A rumor has reached Paris that the Americans have shot down a Soviet plane."

Ariel heard her mother gasp.

"The Soviets claim that the Americans violated Soviet air space and they consider it an act of war. They threaten to launch nuclear missiles in ten hours' time. The United States denies the act and demands a Soviet retraction and apology."

Hugh Marsden said, "Then it is an impasse."

Isaac awoke and began to whimper. "It's all right, son," his father said. "It's all right."

"Girl?" The little boy looked at Ariel. Then, cradling Gladly even more closely, he said, "Mine bear."

"He's not your bear, Isaac," Aaron gently reminded

his son, glancing at Ariel. "He's Ariel's bear. Remember? She has let you have him for a while, but he is her bear. Not yours. Hers."

Isaac buried his face in Gladly's fur. "Mine bear," he said again.

When he looked up, Ariel saw tears on his cheeks. She felt like crying herself, but she knew what she had to do. What she wanted to do.

"It's all right, Isaac," she said. "He's your very own bear now. You'll take good care of him for me, won't you? And may I tell him good-bye?"

Isaac handed the bear to Ariel. It seemed to her that she had not touched him for a long time. She whispered, "You're going to be Isaac's bear now, but I'll always love you." And she gave him back to the little boy.

Isaac reached for Gladly. He kissed the bear. "Mine bear, Girl. Mine bear." And he licked the tears which fell on his lips.

"Yes, he's your bear." Ariel felt her mother's hand on her shoulder, pressing it three times in their private *I Love You* signal.

"Ariel," Isaac's father said, "I do not quite know how to thank you, but I do."

"It's all right, Mr. Steiner," she said. *I guess it's time for me to start growing up,* she thought. And she reached into her pocket to touch the sanctuary knocker.

26

"What do we do now, Uncle?" Jacques asked. Ariel thought he sounded either angry or frightened. She couldn't quite decide which. As for herself, she was frightened.

"We try to compose ourselves for the night," Father André said. "Boys, will you help me for a moment?"

"May I help, too?" Ariel asked.

"And I?" Anne-Marie left her mother to stand near Ariel.

"Yes. Come." The priest led the children into the area where the supplies were stored. When they had seen them before, Ariel had wondered when and how they would be used. Now she knew. Father André pointed to a stack of air mattresses and said, "We do not have sleeping bags, but we have mats and blankets for everyone. Let us carry them out. Also, down farther around this bend are chemical toilets."

"If this crypt were wider, we could put our mats in a circle, as in your American Westerns, Ariel," Jacques said. "Then we could wait for the Indians. Except that we have no guns and the enemy is not Indians."

"Come on, Jack," Christophe said, "don't be so gloomy. This may end peacefully, you know."

"And then again . . ." Jacques began.

"Please, Jacques," Anne-Marie touched his arm, "we must continue to hope. We must! Father André, you said that we are rather like Noah and his family, here in our ark of stone. Noah knew that his world would be destroyed because God told him so. He also knew that he and his family and animals would be safe. Are we here because, even if the world is to be destroyed, we would be safe?"

Before Father André could answer, Jacques broke in. "Maybe we'd be safe, and maybe we would not. I told you, Anne-Marie. Remember? But, Uncle, what I don't understand is why we're here at all. There must be thousands of people, millions, just as worthy of safety as we are. More so. Why us? What about all those others?"

"I cannot answer your question," Father André admitted. "Some questions have no answers. Mr. Herauld told us of others throughout the world in places of safety, as we are. As for the others who are not, I do not know." He sounded sad.

Ariel thought of Brother Michael and his group at Durham; of Mr. Allison and his family somewhere in Nicaragua. And she remembered the very first time she saw the cathedral. It had reminded her of a great ship. *I wish Robin were here,* she thought. *I wonder if she'd be safe in that cellar under the church in Nebraska.*

As she helped with the mats, Ariel glanced at her parents standing apart with the other adults. Their faces were grim. They spoke together so quietly that she could not hear what they said. Tentacles of fear moved along her body.

Before long the mats and blankets had been put in place and the twelve had grouped themselves in the small space.

"Now what, Uncle?" Jacques asked.

"Now we wait."

The gloomy crypt was lit only dimly. Shadows took on eerie forms. Isaac whimpered, clutching Gladly and nestling into his father's arms. Ariel felt anxiety all around her, as dense as fog. She could almost touch it.

Jacques' voice was low, quavery, and intentionally frightening when he said, "Nine hours till doomsday."

"Please, Jacques," Father André said. "What good does this kind of attitude accomplish? Think of Isaac. Surely you do not want to frighten him any more than he is already frightened?"

Jacques had the grace to look ashamed. "I'm sorry," he muttered.

Irina Petrovna asked, "I must know. Do you all consider me to be the enemy? Because I am Russian?" Her pale face was even more colorless in the deep gloom of the crypt.

"No!" Chris was quick to answer. "No, of course we do not consider you to be an enemy. Nobody who can make music as you do could possibly be an enemy."

"Have we made you feel that we are against you, Miss Petrovna?" Hugh Marsden asked.

"No, I truly do not feel that," she answered, "But I need to hear you say aloud that you understand that I desire peace as ardently as all of you desire it."

Julian said, "This may not seem relevant, but I would like to remind you that the other Julian, the one for whom I am named, believed that there is a great plan for all people, a plan we have not made, but a larger plan. And she believed that in the long run, good would be stronger than evil, and that all things would ultimately work together for good. That is what I believe, too. But perhaps not enough of us have had the faith and courage to help bring this about. God needs us to cooperate with Him."

"It's pretty late to start now," Jacques said, looking at his watch. "Less than nine hours to go."

"But, Jacques," Anne-Marie's mother said, "don't you see? Even now we must hope, no matter how late it seems. We must not give up. We must not say that we allow darkness to win."

"I can't bear it," Jacques said. "You people are so unrealistic. All this sweetness and light when in reality we are doomed. I can't bear it."

"Mine bear." Isaac's voice came from the gloom.

Ariel laughed out loud. "Oh, Isaac," she said, "I love you. I really do!"

She heard Isaac's laughter following her own. "Girl," he said. "Mine bear."

"Laughter in the midst of despair," Aaron Steiner said. "Laughter and love. Both are redemptive. Ariel, I thank you."

"What do you really think will happen, Irina?" Emilie Marsden asked. "You are in a better position than any of us to read the minds of your countrymen."

"I do not know," the Russian woman said hesitantly. "I believe, however, that if one of our planes has, in fact, been shot down, terrible things will follow. It will not matter then who has shot it down."

"If the Russians use nuclear bombs, America will, too, will it not?" Christophe asked.

"I'm afraid that's inevitable," Hugh Marsden said.

"Oh, Hugh." Ariel's mother clutched her husband's arm. "It must not happen. It simply must not."

Ariel remembered her dream. Her home gone, her oak tree blackened and dead. She reached for the sanctuary knocker in her pocket and held it so tightly that it cut into her hand. It was supposed to bring her courage. But she began to cry. She couldn't help it. She was afraid.

Part of her heard her parents' words, trying to comfort her in spite of their own distress. Another part of her listened to Alix Leclerc say over and over again, "*Oh Ciel. Ciel!*" as Anne-Marie clung to her.

She heard Aaron Steiner as he chanted words she did not understand.

She heard Jacques cry, "Our parents, Chris. We'll never see them again. I know we won't."

She felt that she was living a nightmare. She tried to imagine whole cities vanishing, destroyed by explosion and fire. It would be as Mr. Long had described it. As it had been in her dream.

Her home gone.

Her tree never to sing again.

Robin's home destroyed. And Robin?

Los Angeles, San Francisco, the great cities of the world in ruins.

Places she had never seen? She would never see them, now.

The pyramids of Egypt, the Acropolis in Athens.

And Chartres, the great stone ship in which they were hiding.

Brother Michael and Durham.

Never again?

She was surprised to hear her own voice crying out, "It mustn't happen. It can't. I don't understand it, not any of it. Why did Mr. Herauld make us come here? To die in this crypt? Why are all those others gathered in places around the world? Like Durham?" Her heart skipped a beat as she thought of her lost friend, Aidan, and of Brother Michael. "What are we supposed to do?"

Emilie Marsden tried to soothe her daughter. "Honey, there's nothing we can do. We just have to wait."

"I don't believe it." Ariel lashed out at her mother. "We weren't brought all this way for nothing. Mr. Herauld wouldn't have done that."

"Well, *chèrie*, do you have a magic wand?" Jacques sounded scornful.

"No, of course I don't have a magic wand." She jumped up and stood facing the others. "But we do have something. We all love our planet and each other. I think we ought to tell God that."

"Just in case He doesn't know?" Jacques' irony cut Ariel.

But before she could answer him, Christophe said, "She's right, Jack. If you can't be helpful, be quiet."

Father André's tone was gentle. "What do you want us to do, Ariel?"

Ariel was close to tears as she answered, and her voice shook. "You know a lot more than I do. All of you grown-ups do. I'm not wise. But I do know that God listens when we talk to Him. He promised. So I think each one of us should do it. Here, now, together. Please. Let's try."

"Yes. Let us join hands." Aaron Steiner's strong voice spoke into the darkness.

Ariel took her parent's hands. They felt warm and strong.

Again Mr. Steiner spoke. "Lord God of Abraham, Isaac, and Jacob, we pray You to hear us in our despair. Maker of the Universe, spare us, that we may live to serve You in peace."

After a long silence, Father André said, "Merciful Father, we earnestly pray that You will send us peace and the wisdom to maintain it. Strengthen our courage to love our neighbors as ourselves as our Lord has taught us." Father André's pleading voice sent shivers through Ariel.

She spoke next. Her words rushed out, tumbling over each other. "Dear God, we love the wonderful world You have given us. We love the sunsets and rain and snow. We love the ocean and the clouds and monkeys and goldfish and . . ."

While she paused for breath, Anne-Marie broke in, "And our cathedral which was built to Your honor and glory."

"And music," Chris said. "Music to make, to share, to enjoy. We can't bear to lose it all."

"Mine bear," Isaac said cheerfully.

After a ripple of soft laughter, Ariel's father spoke. "We beg You to forgive us our blindness. Spare us and teach us to serve You more faithfully."

One by one the others added their prayers. When they had finished, Ariel prayed softly, "Please, God, don't destroy the world. And please let the trees sing again."

At last they all lay down. Ariel lay on her mat, her parents on either side of her, wondering what would happen. *I'll never be able to sleep,* she thought.

"Good night, darling," her father whispered. "Try not to be afraid."

"I'll try, Daddy."

"Good night," her mother whispered. "I love you. Now try to sleep."

"I'll try," she said again. She closed her eyes.

Then, spiraling into the darkness of the crypt came the music of Irina's flute. Ariel sighed with pleasure and rested on the music as if it were a carpet of soft grass. *Maybe Julian's right,* she thought. *Maybe it won't happen.* And holding Brother Michael's sanctuary knocker, she drifted off into a dream in which she was very young. She sat in her tree, high in its sheltering branches, waiting for it to sing.

27

When Ariel opened her eyes again it was morning. Her watch said seven o'clock, although there was little light in the crypt. For just a moment she did not know where she was. Then she remembered. *Maybe this is the last day of the world,* she thought. She shivered and looked around. The others were awake, speaking softly to each other. Ariel, embarrassed, went to use the toilet. She didn't like it. *I guess I'll have to pretend it's a camping trip,* she thought.

Her parents greeted her when she came back. "Not much fun, is it?"

"No, but I'm glad somebody thought of it." Ariel looked across at Christophe who stared into space. She could not catch his eye.

Father André sat at the shortwave radio, but only static and snatches of weather news came into the crypt, and voices speaking in languages which Ariel could not understand. At last a man spoke in French. Father André listened carefully and then turned off the set.

"What did he say?" Ariel asked.

"Only that there is nothing yet. The Soviet Union is silent."

"Perhaps they will not speak at all," Irina Petrovna said. "Perhaps they will only act."

"Meanwhile," Father André said, "let us have our

breakfast." Ariel thought he was forcing himself to sound cheerful.

Ariel's mother, Aaron, and Julian went to help the priest. Ariel sat with Isaac, who leaned against her, rubbing sleep from his eyes. He held Gladly. Soon the others returned with paper plates and cups. Juice was poured from cans, and crackers and hard cheese were served to everyone. "An unusual breakfast, perhaps," Alix Leclerc said, "but nourishing." Ariel was surprised to find that she was hungry.

As they sat together eating, Jacques said, "I want to know about Mr. Herauld. We've talked about him and we can't understand who he is or what he can be, Uncle. He's impossible, and yet, there he is."

"Must everything be proved to you, Jacques?" Julian's voice held a touch of amusement. "Can you take nothing on faith?"

"I can't believe in a man who can be in New Mexico and California and Ohio and Chartres and Heaven knows where else, all at the same time," Jacques insisted. "It's too much to ask of a rational human being. Maybe he was just an illusion. Maybe we all suffered from a kind of mass hypnosis."

"He's no illusion," Christophe said to his brother. "And we all know what he did, that day in June. What we don't know is how he did it."

"And who he really is," Ariel said.

"Jacques," Father André said, "do you believe in this shortwave radio?"

"Of course."

"Can you see the energy which brings the voices to us?"

"You know I can't."

"Still, you believe in that energy and those voices?"

"Yes. I hear the voices, even though I can't see the energy. It's not a fair comparison."

"No? Well, let us try another. Do you believe that your parents exist?"

"Uncle, don't be ridiculous."

"Do you believe in them?" the priest insisted.

"Yes."

"But at this instant you cannot see them."

"Right. But I know they are there. I see what you are trying to do, but it doesn't work. Mr. Herauld is a different matter. He got us all here together, in some mysterious way, and now we're waiting for something to happen. Probably something awful. And where is Mr. Herauld? Who is he trying to fool now?"

"Jack," Christophe sounded stern. "He wasn't trying to fool us. He was warning us. He must have thought something could be done or he wouldn't have brought us all this way. People wouldn't be gathered together in little groups like ours all over the world, the way he said they are, if it wasn't important."

"Do you not think, André," Aaron Steiner asked the priest, "that we, the people of the twentieth century, are unable to accept that which we cannot prove? I think young Jacques is not alone in this attitude. We believe that the age of miracles is past. We are intensely practical. We accept only that which we can contact with our senses. We need to touch, taste, smell, see, hear before we can believe."

"And yet," Ariel's father said thoughtfully, "more and more scientists are accepting the validity of events which cannot be explained in ordinary terms. The transmission of thought waves, for example. Or highly implausible events like similar or identical dreams. Things which do not fall into the category of natural law. We don't know everything."

Father André said, "Exactly. We cannot know everything. Some things we are required to accept on faith. We are not necessarily in control. And now, Christophe, let us try again to see if there is news. Only an hour remains of the designated time."

"The hour of doom and destruction," Jacques said gloomily.

It seemed to Ariel that they all held their breath as Christophe slowly turned the dials. At last she heard and recognized the voice which they had listened to the night before—the French announcer. He spoke rapidly and Ariel wished she could understand what he said. When he had finished speaking, Alix Leclerc burst into tears. Anne-Marie put her arms around her mother.

It's all over, Ariel thought. *It's going to happen.* She looked at Christophe, at all the others who had understood. She could not read their faces. They looked stunned.

It was Irina Petrovna who spoke. "God be praised," she said, "if there is a God. Many of my people say there is not. But I am not so sure. One of our planes crashed, it is true. But that plane was not shot down. Survivors have told the rescuers what actually happened."

Ariel found that she was holding her breath.

"Please tell everyone, Irina," Ariel's father urged.

"It is so hard to grasp," the Russian woman said. "Such a miracle. The plane carried my country's Secretary-General and several members of his bureau. There was a terrible storm. The plane was struck by lightning. It plunged to earth and crashed. The Secretary-General was among the few survivors, but he was injured. They do not say how seriously, of course. It was an assumption only that the Americans had shot down the plane. It is the kind of groundless propaganda in which some of my countrymen specialize."

"Then we're safe?" Ariel asked. "Really safe? The world is safe?"

"Yes." Irina Petrovna shook her head in wonder. "But do you know what else this means? It means that

my father will be in a position of real leadership now,
at least for a while. He will represent my country at the
Geneva meeting. I know that he will find ways in which
to accomplish some of his own plans. The world has a
reprieve. A reprieve from this awful threat of nuclear
catastrophe."

For a few moments, there in the gloom of the crypt,
tears and laughter mingled until Ariel could not tell
who laughed and who cried. *Oh, Brother Michael,* she
thought, *maybe I'll see you again after all. And Robin.
I'll see you when I get home.*

"Thank God! Thank God." The words were whispered, spoken, shouted as the group in the crypt realized that their prayers had been answered.

"Now, let us go up into the light," Father André said.

They followed the winding way through the darkness up into the cathedral. Morning light streamed
through the windows, and Isaac ran about trying to
catch the prisms.

Anne-Marie whispered to Ariel, "My cathedral. I
have been so worried about it. Now I believe it will
stand here forever."

They walked together out into the fresh, clean air of
the cathedral garden. Ariel took a deep breath. Everything smelled new and sweet.

Then she saw him. Mr. Herauld leaned against one
of the trees, smiling at them.

"Mr. Herauld," she called. "You've come back."

Isaac ran toward him with his loose, awkward steps.
"Light," he said, touching Mr. Herauld. "Light." Then
he held up Gladly. "Light, mine bear."

Mr. Herauld scooped up the little boy in a great hug
and then put him down again.

"So," he said to the group. "So, you have another
chance, after all."

"You knew we would, didn't you?" Jacques asked.
"Now please tell us who you really are."

Mr. Herauld looked solemn as he answered Jacques. "I did not know what would happen. I knew only that where willing people seek their way out of darkness, a way can be found. And I am exactly what my name implies."

"A messenger," Christophe said.

"But whose messenger?" Jacques demanded.

Mr. Herauld smiled as he said, "Jacques, Jacques. Can you not take me as I am and ask no more questions?" He turned to Ariel. "And you, my dear young friend, what do you think of all this?"

"I think that there have been enough wars. Too many. There mustn't be any more. We came too close today. Pretty soon we'll be adults, and it will all be up to us. I think that the children of the world have to study other ways. We've got to work toward peace. There must be ways. There must be things we can do. If Irina's father believes it, and if our President really does want peace, there have to be ways."

"And you will find them." Mr. Herauld touched Ariel's shoulder. "Young people will work together until they help to find the path to lasting peace.

"Ariel, do you remember when, at home, you and your friends formed a circle and prayed for peace?"

"Yes. But how do you know about it?"

Mr. Herauld merely smiled. "Is it so different here?" he asked. "All over the world, as I have told you, good, peace-loving people like you are asking God to spare the world which He has made. Do you not believe that these prayers have power? If they continue, with thanksgiving, with faith and good works, who knows what will happen? It may not be too late after all."

For a time the group stood together without speaking. And then Ariel noticed the largest tree, the tree against which Mr. Herauld had been leaning. She watched as it began to tremble and sway, although there was no wind. Light touched the branches and they sparkled as if they were covered with dew or with ice or with diamonds. And the tree began to sing.

Christophe stepped up to stand by Ariel. He took her hand and Anne-Marie joined them. Jacques, looking bewildered, stared into the branches. He took Anne-Marie's hand. Isaac danced around the tree, laughing up at it.

The adults stood as if caught in a dream.

"Oh, Mr. Herauld," Ariel said, "why is it singing? What does it say?"

"The tree sings for joy," Mr. Herauld said. "It sings because there is goodness and beauty and hope in the hearts of children. It sings because it cannot help itself."

"But it sang when Aidan died," Ariel said. "How could it have been happy then?"

"What do you think, Ariel?" Mr. Herauld's eyes were full of love and compassion.

She remembered the look of shining happiness on Aidan's face at the moment of his death. "He wasn't afraid," she said. "The tree sang because Aidan wasn't afraid and because he knew that something wonderful was going to happen to him. Aidan knew." She felt tears running down her face.

Mr. Herauld bent to wipe them away. "You knew that before," he said, "but you did not know that you knew. Now you will never forget."

When Emilie Marsden spoke it was as if she had just wakened from a dream. "Everything looks so new. It's as if I had never seen the sky before."

They walked to the front of the cathedral. Ariel looked up at Princess Emilie where she stood smiling her secret little smile. *I'll be back*, she promised. *Someday I'll be back.*

Standing at the west door together they looked at each other. It was as if no one could believe all that had happened to them. Then Jacques said quietly, in his droll way, "Well, I told you so, didn't I? We've heard everything." He spoke so that the adults could not hear him. "A man who isn't possible. Trees that sing." For a moment he looked solemn and thoughtful. But then he added, "It all came out right, didn't it? I told you it would. I told you so."

"*You* told us so? Jacques, you are impossible," Anne-Marie scolded.

"I know. But lovable?"

Anne-Marie blushed.

"Will you all please come for dessert and coffee tonight?" Ariel's mother spoke to the group. "We must talk together once more before we go our separate ways."

"Will we be leaving soon?" Ariel asked her mother.

"Yes. Very soon."

Ariel glanced at Christophe. Would she ever see him again?

"Light?" Isaac sounded sad. "Light?"

They looked around them, but Mr. Herauld was not there. "He's gone, Isaac," Ariel told the little boy. "He's gone. Maybe we'll see him tonight." But she did not think they would.

28

Once again, as they had on the night of Ariel's birthday, the group gathered at the Marsdens' house. *So much has happened,* Ariel thought. *It seems as if my birthday was years ago. I wonder what will have happened by the time I'm fourteen.*

As they sat together looking at each other, it seemed to Ariel that each person was thinking deep, private thoughts. She broke the silence to ask, "Daddy, Mother said that we'll be leaving soon. When? And are we going straight home?"

"We leave tomorrow," her father said. "We go back to Durham first and then we fly home from London."

In spite of her sadness at the thought of leaving Chartres, Christophe, and her new friends, Ariel felt a lift of joy. She touched the sanctuary knocker in the pocket of her white dress, knowing that she'd touch the real one soon. "I'll see Brother Michael again," she said. "And can we go to Lindisfarne?" She wanted to look at the North Sea and tell Aidan good-bye one last time. She felt that perhaps the cold wind, the water, and the gulls could take him messages.

"I'm sure we can," Emilie Marsden told her daughter. Ariel felt that her mother knew what she was thinking.

"And you, Jacques and Christophe," Hugh Marsden asked the twins. "What happens next for you?"

"We'll spend the rest of the summer here with Uncle

André," Jacques explained. "And our father is to be all of next year at the California Institute of Technology in Pasadena, California. We will live there. Is that city anywhere near your home?"

Ariel looked at Christophe and said, "Oh yes. We'll practically be neighbors."

Christophe did not speak, but his eyes told Ariel, *We will be more than neighbors to each other, you and I.*

Ariel shivered, but not with fear. Suddenly she knew that part of her childhood was over, that she really was growing up.

"And, Aaron," Father André asked, "what is in the future for you, my friend?"

Aaron Steiner held Isaac and Isaac held Gladly. "Now that we have a future, I wish to use it wisely. Julian and I have begun to formulate some plans. We hope to establish a place where children like this one" —he hugged Isaac—"may receive the best possible care in a loving environment. Julian is, as Mr. Herauld told us, a healer of both bodies and souls. She will guide us in our work. We will bear the burdens together."

"Mine bear," Isaac said.

Julian laughed. "Yes, Isaac. We all love you and your bear. And now, no matter what happens, we will do our work and try to believe that *all will be well.*" Looking at Ariel she asked, "Do you remember?"

"Yes. The other Julian. Oh, Julian, do you think you and I will ever see each other again?"

"I'm sure of it. You have to visit Isaac and Gladly, don't you?"

"Alix," Emilie Marsden said, "I know your home is here in Chartres, but we hope that you will come and visit us one day. Ariel could show Anne-Marie what our part of California is like."

"And I will help." Jacques grinned at Anne-Marie. "I shall endeavor to become an excellent guide."

This time Anne-Marie did not blush. She grinned back at Jacques.

She's growing up too, Ariel thought. "You have to come," she told her friend. "You and Robin have to meet. You're my best friends."

"Merci." Anne-Marie looked pleased. "Perhaps one day that will come true. I hope so."

"And you will come back to Chartres," Alix Leclerc said. "We will not lose each other. We have shared too much ever to forget one another."

Father Andre smiled as he said, "And we trust that our cathedral will stand as it has stood. For centuries."

Before anyone could ask Irina Petrovna about her plans she took her flute from its case and began to play. The music rose and fell, binding the friends together in a chain of silver tone. She did not need to speak. Ariel felt her throat tighten. Once again her eyes met those of Chris, and each knew what the other was thinking.

When the last sound had died away Aaron Steiner said, "Irina, I thank you. You have reminded us that where music exists there is joy. And where joy exists, good things are possible. But now once again I must break the spell and take this one to his bed." He hugged Isaac, who grinned his lopsided smile. Everyone stood, preparing to leave.

Isaac said, "Down, Papa." Standing before Ariel he commanded, "Girl. Kiss good-bye."

Ariel bent to kiss the little boy's cheek.

Then he held up Gladly. "Kiss mine bear."

Ariel held Gladly once more, feeling his soft fur. "Good-bye," she whispered to him, the companion of her childhood.

When she looked up Aaron Steiner was smiling down at her. "You are a good friend, Ariel Marsden. Now go and keep the world safe."

Ariel laughed. "I can't do it alone. But I know where I can get lots of help. And I promise to try."

She was sure that the life which stretched before her would be full of surprises. At home, when Christophe came, she would show him her oak tree. Perhaps it would sing. She would never stop listening for it.

Scarcely able to contain her excitement and her joy, she looked around her at her parents and her new friends. "Isn't the world beautiful?" she said. "Isn't it wonderful to be alive?"